The Daughters

Deanna Dickinson McCall

Dedication

Much has been written about the Dust Bowl and men who came to California beginning as early as 1920. By 1950, an estimated one-quarter of all persons born in Oklahoma, Texas, Arkansas, or Missouri, had moved to the West. The culture that developed had deep ties to the traditions from the rural Mid-South and Southwest regions. Much of that culture had its roots in farming and ranching.

My father's family came out from Texas and survived the horrific conditions. My husband's family came out from Oklahoma. Like many veterans who don't discuss their role in war, the grueling travel out West and their arrival's early conditions wasn't a topic of discussion. But, we knew who our people were and where they came from.

So I dedicated this book to honor the women who were the daughters and granddaughters of these hardy people. They flourished despite the bigotry and stigma of having Okie parents and grandparents. The traditions and values passed down to them are still evident today.

Acknowledgments

I would like to thank my readers for hanging in there and waiting for this book to finally appear. You make it worth all the effort it takes to get a book in print, and I cannot thank you enough.

Flint Hemsted's mother, June Hemsted, graciously offered me the use of some of her wonderful photos several months before publication. Before the book could be published, we lost Flint Hemsted. He was my husband's oldest friend, and we feel his loss every day. I know he would be happy and proud to see this book with his mother on the cover.

I also need to thank Evelyn and the editors at White Bird Publications for hanging in there through the pandemic. Evelyn's patience and perseverance are phenomenal.

I would like to thank the folks who read the book, and offered their remarks. Andy Wilkinson and John Dofflemyer, you are especially appreciated!

Last, but, certainly not least, I thank the family and friends I grew up with and gave me the inspiration to tell this story. You are a vital part of the fabric that wove this story.

The Okies' Daughters

White Bird Publications

The Beginning

Me

The subject of the email read *45th Reunion* or I wouldn't have bothered to open it. The link took me to a social media page. I couldn't help but grin. So, they want to have a reunion. That ought to be damn interesting. It had been over forty long years since high school in that little sleepy town. Horses, boys, and cows are what kept us together, and in that order. The social media group I'd been invited to join had all our photos, the current ones, alongside high school black and whites. I didn't feel as bad after seeing some of the "current" photos.

I attempted to wash the dust off my sweaty face and the grit out of my squint lines and other wrinkles.

The only non-dirty place was my forehead. My hat protected it. After scrubbing until my skin hurt, I discovered one spot wasn't dirt.

An age spot. I'd fit right in.

We'd all aged "appropriately." Except for Lori. Her face looked wrinkle-free along with that perfect rodeo queen/cheerleader smile. Her lips were much fuller than I remembered. I wondered what it costs to look like that, and how bad that much surgery hurt.

At least I was still in decent shape, though I didn't have a twenty-four-inch waist anymore. I was still close to the same size I was at twenty-one. Yeah, I was chunky in high school, lost it in my twenties and it never returned. Well, maybe a few pounds now that I am in my sixties. Pounds that want to gather around that once small waist.

I study our old group in the various vintage photos, even Gail. The bright eyes of her youth are there, but a certain flatness peeks through. I don't think I am imagining it.

I feel the old stab, the twist in my heart. I will never forget when I heard she'd been found near death. We had argued over a boy, and hadn't spoken since. When I heard she was bleeding internally and needed blood, I went to the hospital. It was too late. She was gone.

It took me a long time to get past that, and I probably am still not totally past it. It has been a painful lesson in words once spoken can't be taken back. They hang there forever. I swallow and look away before moving to the next photo.

Suzy is there. I pull up her social page. In a relationship it says, married. I heard she had gotten into drugs, and then cleaned up. It appears food is now her drug of choice. She is very heavy. Round and short instead of stout and short. It also appears there's yet another wealthy man in her life. I see photos of her in tropical places, beautiful homes, and lots of expensive dinners. There are no kids. No family members are in the photos. I wonder if her folks are gone, but that still doesn't explain the lack of kids or even grandkids in any photos.

I click on Peggy's photo next. She's standing in front of a display of artwork for which she's famous. I saved the very first piece she gave me, a greeting card she made. Her work is in galleries around the country, even around the world now. Peggy always gave a hundred percent, to school, to rodeo, to everything. Her goal was to please everyone in life since pleasing her mother was not possible. There are pictures of her with horses. I'd judge from the photo…she's still got nice horses. She looks happy and confident. I am glad.

Now for Donna, the only one I've seen at all in a long time. The profile picture has not been doctored at all. Her face is thin. The round cheeks are gone. Long creases line the once pink plump cheeks. I see the story of a battle, of a hard life written on her face, and the earlier skirmishes of alcoholism. There seems to be a certain vulnerability reflected in the photo. She was always the first to agree to do a dare and was never afraid of anything. I wonder what part of life finally taught her fear. She's still got horses and some mules. I see her with them in the photos. Only Donna would have mules. I chuckle.

An old group photo comes next on the website from an FFA competition. Someone has written on the photo "Virginia always wins!" with an arrow pointing to me. Following the FFA photo are some rodeo and horse show photos, most in black and white. I am guessing all the old photos came from our yearbooks, and from the old rodeo and horse show photographers.

We were girls on stocky, short quarter horses with too much muscle for the tiny feet under them. I think I can tell the Wranglers are colored, and some are checked rather than denim blue as in some of the earlier photos. We paired them with fitted shirts that have big sleeves that balloon out. Women's Wranglers hadn't been invented yet; we pegged the legs and darted the waists until we decided a couple of years later they looked better without the alterations. We no longer had to endure the heavy darts digging into our waists until we bled. We learned about freedom of movement and looking natural, wearing men's jeans. Tall, crowned hats, flat-heeled roper boots, or boots with exotic leather wingtips and buck-stitching, along with over-sized sunglasses, completed our idea of looking California cool.

Our parents and grandparents considered us spoiled rotten. We had no conception of what our parents and grandparents had endured to get to the Promised Land of California. That part of their lives wasn't discussed much.

We were their daughters. The Okies' daughters.

PART ONE

The Early Years

Deanna Dickinson McCall

Chapter One

Me

The Farm Bureau meeting is held at the old Grange Hall. I smell the waxed floors and other odors, perhaps the mustiness of old books. I smell the food, too, and my tummy grumbles. I hide behind either my daddy or Granny. I am not used to so many people and so much bustling around. There are young families in attendance. Men wearing straw hats and short sleeved plaid western shirts with pearl snaps, Levis are cuffed above cowboy boots with slanted riding heels. Some of the men have children perched on a jutting hip. The women flit about in flowered print dresses with fitted waists and flowing skirts, which they probably made. They set food out and shoo older children out of the way with directions to go play. A few of the women wear what they call dungarees with dainty, pointed toe boots or saddle oxfords. Some of the bolder women wear straw cowboy hats on hair that was set in rollers and dried.

The older generation is here, too. My family refers to them as "The Real Farmers." They wear "Farmer" hats and bib overalls, along with brogan shoes. Some of the stockmen wear smaller brimmed hats, shirts with bolo ties, and slacks above polished boots. These men are mostly the older fathers and grandfathers of those present and carry themselves with dignity.

No important business happens here, though the men all sit through a meeting, make motions, and second them, following the tattered book of Robert's Rules and Order. It is a meeting of reassurance in many ways, of traditions they want continued, though I don't understand this until I am an adult.

Most of the food lined up on the long tables is home grown, everything from meats to beans and vegetables, to pies and cakes. Some of the women comment on what they brought for the feed; a mess of green beans, fried chicken, and chocolate pie topped with meringue, which the men call calf slobbers, and cat head or baking powder biscuits. Hawaiian punch will be served to all, pronounced Ha-why-in. My Granny always brings sweet tea, too.

The men all know that they will be "eating high on

the hog." Many of the other children play together, while waiting for the call to pray before dinner. I watch some little girls, too young to attend school, who are eyeing me and some other little girls. They twist pieces of their hair around their fingers and rotate their small ankles while pointing their toes. I am one of the ones being scrutinized. Some are wearing dresses and ribbons, have patent leather shoes, and white anklet socks. I am among the few girls wearing cowboy shirts and jeans with boots. The other girls in the cowboy clothes imitate horses, skipping and neighing.

I watch them, wanting to join in. I can see the daintier girls wish they could be galloping around instead of worrying about lace and hair ribbons. One of the cowboy-girls approaches them and takes their hands, leading them into the circle to join the loping and neighing herd of make-believe. They toss their hair like manes, and some stomp their feet in the age-old ritual of little girls imitating horses. One little girl in a ruffled dress comes to me and draws me into the circle. I am free to join, to toss my mane, and stomp my feet in time. I have become gathered into the herd at last.

The pickup can be heard coming down the new road cut into the hillside of the canyon. I know the man who made the road; his name is Ring-Tail. Granddaddy says he earned that name on account of how he drives that big ol' dozer. Says he's crazy as a ring-tailed cat.

I'm only four years old, but I recognize the sound of the truck's gears. Daddy's coming back to the house after putting out the Beefy-16 feed supplement and salt blocks. I didn't get to go this time. I love to lick the loose feed and the salt. Granddaddy says I will get run over one day doing that, that a bull or cow will get me for eating their food. Sometimes they come after me, swinging their big heads. Our McNabb dog, named Poncho, stops them. I've spent the day with Granny while she cooks, instead.

Mama comes home from teaching school. She is as unhappy as always, snapping at me, fussing about my daddy getting home to start the generator so she can get things done. Our only power comes from the old generator in the shed that has to be cranked and cranked 'til it starts.

I slip and say son-of-a-gun in front of her, and she says Granny shouldn't talk that way in front of me, much less let me say it. Mama doesn't like or approve of Granny, even I know that. Mama has changed out of the homemade flowered dress she wore to teach school and put on a plaid shirt and loose jeans. She rolls the too long legs up and that shows her white socks and oxford shoes. I hate shoes. I wear boots every day, whether I am in a dress or my jeans. I love wearing boots, and I have to wear them because of the snakes. My newest boots have beautiful butterflies on the top, their colorful wings spread wide. I admire them several times a day. Granddaddy says they are good boots, but not as good as his Paul Bonds.

I run past the pallet that our hired hand, Hank, sleeps on and leap off the old wrap around porch. Hank hasn't come in from town yet, and I hear Granddaddy tell Mama he probably tied one on. I don't know what he ties onto in town. I do know it takes him awhile to untie it and come back, sometimes a few days. He always brings me treats from town, usually candy or a small toy.

I am not allowed to leave the fenced yard. When my family moved here a few months before I was born, seventy-five rattlesnakes were killed in the yard, or real close to the house. Granny says there's a den in the lava rock above the spring that sends water to our house and barn.

When Granddaddy wanted to get some dynamite to use on the den, Daddy told Granddaddy they couldn't risk blowing up the den; it could seal up the spring, and they could lose all the water. The spring also provides all the water for irrigating the bottom of the canyon. So, we live with the snakes. The porch and yard is checked every morning before I can go out to play. One morning after someone checked the yard, I was playing under the fig tree, my favorite place. I heard a buzz and ran inside and got Granny. She grabbed a hoe and killed the snake, buried the head, and threw the rest of it where the wild hogs would come eat it later.

The wild pigs scare me when they come. Some of them have big ol' tusks, and they charge the trees in the old orchard behind the house, trying to knock the fruit or nuts down. They ruin the meadows that Daddy and Granddaddy irrigate, tearing the grass up, so Daddy or Granddaddy shoot at them.

Today I cannot wait to see Daddy to tell him about the candy Granny and I made. It is his favorite, date nut log. I forget about the rattlesnakes and rules in my excitement and go running out the yard gate. He is parking over by the walk-in box where we hang meat and keep food cool that won't fit in the propane refrigerator. I see him climb out of the pickup, and he is watching me running toward him. I see his face turn red with anger, and I remember I am not supposed to be there, not supposed to leave the yard. He grabs one of my arms real tight and swings me in the air, striking my bottom again and again. I try not to cry, but it hurts both my fanny, my feelings, and my arm. He sets me back on the ground hard and yanks me behind him to start walking toward the house. Halfway across the drive, he stops and points, roughly pulling me in front of him. He points at the ground, and I can see anger rising in his face again. I am filled with fear. I follow his finger to see a very small rattlesnake, laying with its head smashed and almost cut off.

"You see that? Your boot heel did that; you didn't

even see it!" Daddy pauses before he continues yelling. "It could have struck you! You weren't even watching! When you are told to stay in the yard, damn it, stay there!"

I hang my head in shame, and follow behind him, watching my boots slowly and carefully cover the ground I am supposed to always watch, the joy of the candy forgotten.

I am now in the second grade and Mama got her way. We have moved off the ranch to a small place. I head down the hallway of the new house Daddy built for Mother, yawning and wondering what Mama would have ready for breakfast. This house is just a few miles outside of town and I don't like living this close to folks.

Mama's sorry cooking is just another reason to miss the foothill ranches and my grandparents. I know breakfast will likely be bland and tasteless. It makes me remember all the stuff I loved living on one of the ranches.

Granddaddy fixes good breakfasts, there are all kinds of good stuff when he cooks, which is usually when there are cattle to be worked. He set the breakfast table too early, though, before the sun was even thinking about coming up. I don't want to eat that early, and the table was always loaded with food. Plates of fried eggs, mounds of sausage and bacon, ham, beef or venison steaks, hot cakes, syrups, biscuits, cream gravy and fresh or canned fruits. Whatever we had, he cooked all of it. When I was old enough to ride and help with the cattle, he made syrup buckets to put in my pocket for later in the day. Granddaddy would stick his thumb in one of his big ol' biscuits and fill it up with syrup, then wrap it in waxed paper so it could be eaten later. Granny taught me to put chocolate powder in the coffee so I could drink it. *The coffee would float a shoe*, Daddy always said. The chocolate flavored coffee was a good change on a cold morning, better than the gritty orange powdered drink I usually had.

Anyway, I hear the radio that always sits on the TV tray playing. Dad always keeps it there so he can listen to the farm and livestock news while he sits at the table and drinks coffee in the mornings. I slide into my seat, and Dad points up at the ceiling.

"You see those damn things? What the hell are they doing, girl?" He shakes his head, staring at the ceiling, plainly confused.

I look at the ceiling and see nothing. I look back at my Dad and realize that something is wrong. His face is different, and his eyes are weird. He has those gray eyes that are like almost not having any color, anyway. I shake my head and say, "No, sir," in a quiet voice. He looks at me, puzzled why I can't see what he sees. I feel weird and try not to squirm.

I try to steal a glance into the kitchen to see what

Mother is doing. She shakes her head at me and then looks away. She stirs oatmeal that will be lumpy and taste like paste. I'm glad I'm not really hungry. Daddy still stares up at the ceiling, watching something I can't see. I don't understand what is happening and am frightened. Mama is doing what she usually does, pretending that nothing is going on, no matter that something is really going on, like when Granddaddy and Daddy are fighting. It is ten years later before I know what the DTs are.

I climb off the school bus, and as soon as I open the door, I hear the yelling. I sneak down the hallway and change into play clothes as quick as I can. I plan to escape to my grandparents, who live across the pasture. Daddy moved them to this little place since the last real ranch is now gone. Daddy just runs some cows on the irrigated pasture that surrounds the new house and goes down to the little house my grandparents live in.

When I walk into my grandparent's front room, Granddaddy is knelt in front of Granny who is sitting on the couch leaning over sideways. He is holding Granny's limp hand while she slowly drags her other hand across her face. Granddaddy is trying to get Granny to answer his questions. I have never seen my grandparents like this, and I am terrified and know something horrible is happening. I run back across the pasture as fast as I can. I run into the house and tug on my Daddy, telling him something is wrong, and that he has to go to Granny and Granddaddy's. Daddy stares at my stricken face, finally grabs his hat, and we jump in the pickup.

I learn that Daddy thinks my beloved Granny has had a stroke. He is very serious and asks Granddaddy and Granny both a lot of questions before he calls for help. I stand back and tremble, wrapping my arms around myself. It is an hour before the ambulance arrives, and I only know that nothing can happen to her. She can't die. My chest hurts from holding in the sobs. We finally follow the ambulance to town. Daddy seems more normal now and looks at me.

"You did right. You probably saved your Granny's life coming to me for help." It is rare praise. I swallow hard and squint to hold back the tears. Granddaddy reaches over, squeezes my arm, and nods in approval.

I am now in junior high and spend most of my time on a horse. I consider myself pretty well schooled, I have learned a lot from girl friends and their parents. I already know about ranch horses. For being "a good cow horse," this one I am on sure moves slow. He picks his way through rocks like they're hot. You'd think he was walking on raw eggs, instead of lava rock that cover a good part of this country. I'm thinking that he seems more like a valley or arena horse.

These folks invited me to ride with them. I need to make a decent showing. I grew up in the rocky foothill country, and that was why I asked to help today. I am supposed to know what I am doing, and know how to ride through the brushy, lava-rock-covered country. I see a cow hide behind an oak tree up ahead and decide old tender foot here needs to get going before the cow hits the manzanita thickets. I lean forward and push the reins ahead a little to get the horse to pick up his pace, but get no response. Alrighty, then. I barely glimpse the cow weaving in and out of the trees and brush. Dang it. I gently apply the old Garcia spurs I am wearing. A long-time family friend gave them to Dad when Mom and Daddy lived down in the Central Valley. It is a privilege to get to wear them. I am told this and to make sure they are wired down, every time I wear them. The old friend's family had been in California forever, and the spurs are old and worth quite a bit of money; besides the fact Dad's old friend has passed away and they have great sentimental value.

The minute the horse feels the spurs he goes berserk, bucking and squealing through the rocks. Oh, man, I hope no one sees this. I try to grab anything and everything on the saddle to help me stay on. The stupid horse squeals like a dang pig, ear-piercing squeals. There's no way this will go unnoticed, to say the least. I have not been on a horse that bucks like this. I've only heard stories of it, and this scares me.

I end up flat on my back on the rocks. There's no place to land that isn't rocks.

The other riders come up, barely suppressing grins. I try to gather what's left of my dignity and slowly get up. I move my head and neck carefully and hear one of them remark it is a good thing I am only twelve. If I had been an adult, I wouldn't be getting up so fast. There are some boys a little older than me in the group, and I look down to see my shirt has become unsnapped and is torn. Great. One of the older men stares at my big ol' spurs and warns me that horse won't take much spurring. I wish he'd mentioned that earlier.

I climb back on and try to reach an understanding with the stupid horse. The headstall they gave me to put on him has split reins. There's no romal to motivate him. He seems to react to a branch I break off better than spurs, once I show him I have it. I make sure to keep the spurs out of him. We finally get the cattle to the corrals after playing hide-and-seek through the brush and trees. I decline to help with the sorting and instead work one of the gates. Maybe the horse can at least do that. He watches the switch I have out of the corner of his eyes.

I am dropped off at my house at the end of the day. My head hurts, and I am sore, but my pride hurts more than anything. I go directly in the garage and open the garbage can. I bury those old big, roweled spurs deep in the can, covering them with empty vegetable cans and other stuff that won't burn. I have wanted those cool, little slip on spurs all the other girls wear, and all I've ever had to wear are those old, heavy things. Now, maybe Dad will buy me some when we "discover" the old ones are missing.

Chapter Two

Suzy

Suzy spends most of her play time in the pen behind the house, even though she is only four years old. The fat little pony stands still while the plump little girl combs his mane. He loves the watermelon she gives him when she comes into his pen, even though it is just the rind. She is supposed to save the rinds for her Granny. She makes sweet, syrupy preserves out of the rind. The dappled pony doesn't mind the attention, but will turn quickly, baring his teeth when the chubby little hands pull too hard on the knots in his mane. Suzy can climb all over him, even stand on his back with nothing on his head or anyone holding him. She loves to do that.

When her mama and daddy catch her in the pen, standing on the pony's back, they look at each other in amazement. A few minutes later they have her try to see if she can spread her arms and balance on one bare foot while the pony stood chewing on his treat. They watch their daughter standing on the pony's back and exchange knowing looks. The little girl with the bronc-rein-thick yellow braid and bright smile sure made a cute picture on the little spotted pony. The crowds would eat it up. They know they will.

They have always been delighted to have a child who loves horses as much as they do. Their son, Luke, has no interest in horses. He lives for baseball and other sports.

"Suzy-girl, how would you like to do this in the rodeo or the parade?" Daddy asks as he pushes his straw hat back off his face.

Suzy's mom smiles, even after she spots the remnants of the watermelon rinds on the ground. Suzy smiles her biggest smile, happy to not be in trouble. Suzy nods, jumps down off the pony, and runs to be hugged by both her parents.

Suzy is quickly enrolled in gymnastic and dance classes to aid in her strength, grace, and balance. Her parents dismiss the coach's concern that Suzy is young for the classes. When she asks to join the local Brownie or church group, her parents tell her she doesn't have time for that. Suzy makes her first appearance in the local rodeo parade. Dressed in pink fringes and sequins, she stands on her pony with bouquets of flowers in each hand. The stock contractor sees the little girl and makes a deal for Suzy to appear that night in the first performance.

Suzy enters the arena standing on her pony. Her feet are slid under the surcingle her daddy had made for her. The crowd loves the little girl, and Suzy's folks are smiling. The clown joines in the applause and announces he will send her first appearance off with a bang. When the firecracker goes off behind the pony, he jumps sideways in fear, and Suzy falls, her feet still wedged under the leather strap. The pony begins to try to run away from the child, flopping at his side. Someone from the Grand Entry runs their horse alongside to help Suzy. Just as he comes alongside, her feet come loose, and Suzy falls under the would-be rescuer's horse's hooves.

The ambulance driver checks the little girl, announcing she has likely sprained both her ankles, could well have a concussion, and needs to see a doctor. Suzy's parents give her some baby aspirin and have her ride the pony bareback out in the arena to show the crowd that she is okay. Suzy swallows her tears and waves at the crowd. Suzy's brother, Luke, watches from the gate and shakes his head at his parents. He feels bad for his little sister, and is disgusted at his parents' behavior.

The gym is warm and the balance beam is slippery. Suzy feels sweat break out on her face. She hopes it doesn't cause another zit. She is one of the shortest girls in the class, but the coach told her she was lucky. Suzy is strong, and all her weight is centered in a smaller area. Plus, Suzy already had good balance and strength from trick riding. Suzy's folks make her take these advanced classes when she finished with the ballet classes. Her muscles ripple with every move, and her arms and shoulders are stronger than most of the boys on the football team. She beat most of them arm wrestling on a regular basis. Her leg muscles match her upper body strength. She is a little powerhouse. Suzy is being sent off to learn new tricks from the best of the best, all the way to Texas, her daddy said. He wants her to be strong and ready to learn. She won't have to stay as long, and it won't cost as much since Suzy is already in shape, and practices all the balancing techniques.

Suzy thinks about the motor home they travel in every weekend now. It was the first Winnebago anyone around there had seen. It is paid for by Suzy's contract act. Her earnings on the circuit are paying for a lot of things. They'd even gone all the way to Hollywood in the Winnebago, where her folks tried to get the movie folks to hire Suzy to do stunts and stuff. The film people told her parents Suzy isn't old enough. They can't hire a kid to do that stuff.

Her folks also tried to get them to do a movie about Suzy. They'd laughed at them and told them to go back to their "farm" and have Suzy come back to try doing stunts when she was done with high school.

Suzy's brother moved in with their aunt and uncle. At least, they were home on the weekends and watched his games. She misses Luke. He goes to the high school next to her junior high school, and sometimes they meet during lunch break. He asks Suzy if she is okay, if she is sore or hurt from all the stuff their crazy folks make her do. Suzy shakes her head no, assures him she is all right, then asks how his games are going and how his grades are. Suzy can't remember the last time Luke has come home and seen her parents. She also can't remember the last time she's heard her parents even mention Luke.

Chapter Three

Peggy

Peggy swings her boots over the edge of the grandstand while she hangs onto the pipe rail in front of the bleachers. She stops when she hears her daddy's name being called. She watches him back his horse, Paycheck, into the corner of the roping box. He has his piggin' string in his teeth and another hoggin' string in his belt. The little horse is raring to go.

Mike holds him poised in place. Peggy knows that little horse will burst out like a rocket when her daddy lets him go. Her mother, Sandy, tells the woman on the other side of her that Mike better win, or at least place. She is tired of all the money he spends on entries, and this is the local Fair rodeo, after all. He doesn't need to disgrace her here, of all places. Peggy claps her hands and hollers for her daddy as he catches the calf and ties it. He always does such a slick job. Peggy is so proud. He walks back to his horse and waves his hat at the crowd in answer to the announcer's spiel about how local folks ought to be proud of her daddy taking first place.

After the rodeo, the crowd gathers around the concession stand to get something to eat. Sandy and Mike stand in line, with Peggy next to them. Peggy is thinking that a burger would be so good, maybe with some chili and cheese on it. A man and his freckled-faced, red haired wife are walking by when they suddenly stop. The woman has a low cut, snug blouse on and wears tight pants with fancy boots.

"Hey, how the heck you been, Mike? Sure was a nice loop you threw." The man shakes Mike's hand, and the woman smiles down at Peggy and her waist length, shiny braids. "And who is this little darlin'?" the woman asks.

"This is my daughter, Peggy. She's six." Mike answers proudly.

"She's a purty lil' thing, and a sure enough throw-back," the woman says, winking at Mike. Peggy's mom, Sandy, clears her throat and steps forward before asking with a snobby note in her voice who they might be, seeing as how her husband had failed to introduce them.

The ice in Sandy's voice is impossible to ignore.

Mike cringes and quickly makes introductions. The woman smiles stiffly at Sandy and turns away, telling her husband they need to be going. The man tips his straw hat at Sandy, who barely nods in return. Peggy feels her mother's anger.

"Who the hell does that poor ol' Okie tramp think she is?" Sandy snarls. "She can't even speak proper English. Whatever Peggy gets in those looks comes from your side. That's coming from your people."

Peggy heard someone call her Mama's folks, her grandparents, Okies, one day, and she knew her mama would have been furious, though she had no clue why. All four of her grandparents had come from Oklahoma. She makes a mental note to look that word, "throwback", up at school. It was the second time someone had said that about her. She is worried. It sure sounds like maybe she should have been thrown back and been replaced with a better kid, like the calves that don't come out of the chute right for her daddy to rope.

The little horse slides to a stop. Peggy pats his sweaty neck. She knows he puts everything he possesses out for her. Roany is all heart, he has always been that way. That was a good run, and she is happy. Roany never lost a beat as he ran between the poles. Her mother motions her over to the webbed lawn chair. "That kind of run won't be winning anything when you start going to the high school rodeos. Time to think about getting rid of old Roany. You're getting too big for him anyway."

Peggy's heart drops. The little Welsh and horse cross gelding had been hers forever, it seemed. He is her best friend. She knows he is getting a little older, but can't imagine not having him in her life. She decides to talk to her Dad before she lets her mom sell him. No way will she allow him to be chickened, she vowed. Roany is too good for that. Maybe one of her younger cousins can take him if she isn't allowed to keep him.

Before supper that evening Peggy is in her room, working on the beading loom her grandmother has given her. She made her friends beaded rosettes for their braided pig tails and was currently working on a hat band. The tiny seed beads work into beautiful patterns, Peggy has mastered the art of making pretty designs, including flowers. Her mother hates it when Peggy wears the rosettes, especially when an announcer said she looked like a little Indian Princess. Her dad stood up to her mother when she tried to make Peggy quit wearing them. Peggy hears her father finally come into the house.

She hears her mother immediately start in about how they need to get rid of Roany if Peggy is going to continue to compete. She goes on to say how high school rodeo and the state association rodeos were a whole different world from junior rodeos.

Like her dad doesn't know this.

Peggy opens her door and slips down the hall to listen. Her mother is telling Mike how he gives in to everything Peggy wants, and she's tired of it. She's taken matters into her own hands by calling the horse trader to come get Roany.

Peggy hears her dad slam his drink glass down and yell at her mother. Tears course down Peggy's face as she prays her dad will call and stop the trader from coming. Why does her mother have to be so hateful?

Chapter Four

Gail

The ditch water runs fast and cold through the emerald green pasture, and the two little girls shiver and squeal with delight. They splash through the water spreading over the field and attempt to jump over the ditch, splashing themselves even more.

"Hey, Gail, let's run all the way down to where the tarp is set and get in where the water is deep," Donna suggests, her impish grin lighting her face.

Gail thinks about the prospect and knows if Donna's daddy catches them, Donna will get a spanking, or worse, but the thought of getting in that pool behind the tarp is such a temptation. It will be deep and still and mysterious to the six-year-old girls.

"Come on, fraidy cat!" Donna yells, running next to the ditch, through scattered white and rose clover and bright yellow dandelions, all buzzing with bees. The placid Hereford cattle chew their cud and watch them with little interest. Gail begins to run after her friend, their bare feet splashing through the water flooding the field. Gail yells in pain and stops suddenly, hopping on one foot. Tears form and splash down her face before Donna turns around to see what is the matter.

"Bee?" Donna asks. Gail's tearful and immediate nod and her quivering bottom lip tell Donna all she needs to know. Donna grabs Gail's hand, pulls her down to sit on the ditch bank, and then looks at her foot. Donna explains that she is going to scrape the stinger out, if it is still there. Gail tries to peer around Donna's head to see what Donna is doing.

"The stinger is gone," Donna announces and reaches into the side of the ditch bank, pulling out a handful of mud, and slaps it on Gail's foot.

"There, that will pull the poison out. That's what my Granny always does when I get stung. We will just sit here for a bit and let that mud dry," Donna says with grave wisdom. Donna always knows what to do, even though the girls are of the same age. Gail would have run home and had her mama take care of it, but when Donna is with her, Donna handles things.

Donna doesn't have a real mama like Gail does,

and Donna's dad was grouchy all the time. Gail is afraid of him and doesn't like to be at Donna's house. Donna's grandparents live there, too, since Donna's mama left. Donna's daddy sometimes has a girlfriend staying there that he tries to make Donna call "Mama." Donna's daddy says that someday Donna would have a new mama, and then she will have to call her "Mama."

Donna refuses to call anyone "Mama," no matter how much trouble and scolding happens. Donna confides to Gail that she will stay in her room forever and get a spanking every day before that happens.

Gail's mama sometimes makes or buys the two girls the same clothes, like they are twins. The girls spend every day playing together, mostly at Gail's house or out in the fields between their homes. Donna loves being at Gail's. They get to make cookies with icing, play games, and do fun stuff. Gail's mama even gave Donna a birthday party last year. It was the first real birthday party Donna could remember. There was a cake with fancy flowers, and it even had writing that said *Happy Birthday*. There were presents, balloons, and games.

Birthdays aren't much at Donna's house. Sometimes whoever has the birthday might get to choose what to have for dinner, something special like a mess of quail or frog legs. Hunting and fishing seasons and licenses don't mean anything to Donna's family. The land and everything that lived on it is theirs, they reckon. The Good Book said it was. There is no disputing that fact.

Gail is the light of her mama's life, and whatever Gail wants, she generally gets. Donna can't remember ever hearing that Gail got into real trouble, never heard of her getting the strap or even a real spanking. Gail even has a pony, one they ride bareback together across the fields until the pony gets tired and bucks them off. Then Donna will jump back on and show him who was boss. Gail always tries hard to keep up with Donna, but Donna is always so brave and strong.

Gail stares in the bathroom mirror, studying her reflection. Her mama is letting her to begin to wear a little make-up. Both her daddy, Waylon, and her brother made fun of her the first time she came out with it on. Her brother pointed and asked no one in particular where the clown came from, that he didn't know there was a circus in town. Then he laughed so hard he liked to have fallen off the couch. Her mama simply told her that she was supposed to use only a little and needed to go wipe most of it off. She decides to try lining her eyes again, but it ends up as a big old circle.

She half halfheartedly listens, eavesdrops, really, to the voices drifting in the window. Her folks and grandparents are sitting out in the yard under the big trees drinking sweet iced tea. They are talking about

Donna's family and when they all came out here to live. She's heard most of this before, but stops messing around with the makeup when she hears their voices drop low. She knows this is something juicy, something she probably isn't supposed to hear. Gail leans into the open window and strains to hear.

Her mother's voice is barely audible. "I understand a teacher finally did something. Poor little Donna—for a daddy to tolerate that. He wasn't that way until his wife left. We all said she must of turned into a tramp, after listening to them. Maybe she wasn't so bad after all. I heard she told someone she saw the writing on the wall and tried to take Donna with her. They threatened her and said they'd tell the police all kinds of things, made-up things if she tried to take Donna."

"I just can't understand Harold or his own damn son. That family was never that way. Lord, we've known them forever." Gail's daddy is speaking a little louder and easier to hear. "When the constable come by, I couldn't hardly believe it. He came figuring we'd have a good idea of what was happening. If I had known what was going on, I'd of sure as hell stopped it. Poor little gal, she is always over here playing with Gail. We knew things weren't good over there after Diane left, but we had no idea that was going on. Makes me sick. Old man deserves to be run outta town on a rail."

Gail wonders what is happening to Donna. She

holds her breath and gets on her tiptoes to hear her daddy better. "Well, at least he is gone. He took off when the constable showed up. I guess that little girl was changing into her gym outfit when the teacher saw some blood on her under panties.

"When the teacher got close, she could smell what had been going on, and when the teacher talked to Donna, she told the teacher that her Granddaddy was always messing with her, telling her he had to make sure she was okay and could have children one day. It's been going on for years, ever since Diane left, come to find out. She didn't know it wasn't right, poor little thing, no mama around. Old man molesting his granddaughter. Good thing we aren't back in Oklahoma. He'd have gone missing a long time ago. Folks won't tolerate that stuff back there and will take care of it themselves. He better not come back, either. For Donna's sake, the less said, the better. She's got a hard-enough row to hoe without folks finding out about this." All of the adults voice their agreement with Waylon.

Gail leans her head against the wall and shudders. She will keep her best friend's secret forever.. she vows. She wraps her arms around herself and silently cries for her friend. Poor Donna. Gail has seen bruises on her arms, and once on her neck, but didn't know anything about this.

Chapter Five

Donna

Donna's Granddaddy Harold studies the old horse she brought up and is tied under the apple tree in the yard. He watches the old horse carefully plod along behind the little girl. The horse begins nosing among the leaves and pulls a branch down to reach an apple hidden among the leaves.

"Don't you let him get at them apples, dadgumit, girl!" He strides over to the horse, unties him and throws the lead rope at Donna's face.

Wide-eyed, Donna stares at her granddaddy, fearful he might slap her. He stares back, looking as if the thought is crossing his mind.

"You have no idea what it is to go hungry, child. I hope to God you never have to know. There was a time your daddy, your Grandmama, and the rest of this family would have given the ragged, only shirt they owned off their back to have had an apple to eat. We ain't feeding those apples to a damn horse."

Donna lowereds her head, shame washing over her. Her grandparents were always preaching *waste not, want not,* at her. She tries hard to not be wasteful, but it seems like she could never be careful enough. When she tries to ask her daddy why they are that way, saving scraps of food and even old bread, he brushes her off. When she asked him why they were so poor when he was a boy, he slapped her across the face and walked away. Donna was discovering the old saying about children, that they should be seen and not heard, was really true.

Donna later figured out her being what her Grandmama called the spittin' image of her long-gone mother, mostly makes her daddy angry. It isn't the questions that she asks. At eight years old, Donna is already getting a chest that will resemble her mother's over abundant bosom. Her granddaddy stares at her chest, and it makes her feel funny. Her grandmother showed her how to wrap her chest with sheets torn into bandages, so they don't stick out so much and get what Granny calls unwelcome attention. She hopes it keeps her granddaddy from checking her all the time to make sure she is okay.

Donna remembers her mother, Diane, a little. She'd run off when Donna was five. She remembered the peroxide blonde hair, the scent of cigarettes, and cheap perfume. Donna thinks her mama looked like a movie star, with her hair all curled and the tight dresses she wore. Donna came home from kindergarten to an empty house one day. The night before, Diane had washed and combed Donna's hair, and when she tucked Donna in, she told her to remember her Mama would always love her. That was the last time Donna saw her. She didn't know if her daddy had seen Diane again, since Donna was most likely the reason her mama ran off. Donna's Grandmama said that isn't the reason, but Donna figures it really is, and that's why she isn't allowed to say anything about her mother or even mention her name. It just makes her daddy madder than ever at Donna.

Donna stares at the ceiling and tries to pretend she is somewhere else. She is glad Gail and Gail's' mama is in the waiting room. The principal and the other folks the school called let them come with Donna. Donna is amazed to find out that Gail knows about her Granddaddy. Gail tells her she isn't telling anyone, anything. Ever. Her secret is safe with her. Then they'd cut their fingers and held them together to make the blood oath stick.

Donna hopes the doctor is a woman. The nurse who had Gail and her mama go to the waiting room is nice, but Donna knows she is looking at her with pity. Donna doesn't want anyone feeling sorry for her.

Donna has already been called in to talk to the school counselor, and they'd said it was okay with the folks from the children's agency at the state for her to stay at Gail's until all of this was settled.

Gail's mama had gone to college to learn about kids and stuff. She quit working to stay home with Gail. That's why they let her stay at Gail's. Gail's mama explained the agency will need to know why Donna has never told anyone about her granddaddy. Why she didn't tell her grandmother or father. Donna had turned her head away. She can't tell them her daddy can't hardly stomach the sight of her, and she's already overheard him say she was just like her mama, a tramp. He is fixing to get married and never pays any mind to Donna nowadays. Donna didn't know for sure what a tramp was when she was younger, back then she thought it was a hobo. She'd thought that's probably where her mama went, on a train or something and couldn't find her way back. Her grandparents were the only ones who ever showed her any affection, and by the time she figured out her granddad's kind of affection probably wasn't right, she no longer cared. At least it was someone who noticed her and hugged her. By then she didn't care if she was a tramp. It didn't matter anymore.

The social worker looks tired and overworked, and is relieved when Gail's mama gives her papers that say she can stay with them. It has already been okayed by everyone that really matters. Donna doesn't know what is gonna happen, and she is scared.

Everyone ask about her mother, and Donna tells them she hasn't heard from her in years, not even at Christmas-time. Donna hears the social worker tell the principal that Okies do this kind of stuff all the time. That's why sometimes the kids have six toes, or other things are wrong with them, like being retarded. She wishes Gail's mama had heard them say that. She'd have set them straight. That kinda talk makes Gail's mama angry.

Donna put on the gown and climbs back up on the table. She closes her eyes and hopes no one at school knows why she was pulled out of class and why she is staying at Gail's until this is all settled.

Chapter Six

Lori

Lori sits very still while her mama carefully ties the pink bow in her hair and sprays the curls. It is hard to breath when the hairspray fills the air, and Lori holds her breath as long as she can. Today is Picture Day, and she has on one of her new dresses that her mama made for her. She loves to go with her mama to pick out the material for her dresses at the variety store. There are all kinds of pretty, flowered prints, ribbons, and laces to choose from. Her mama will study the picture on the pattern envelope and sometimes even draws a copy of the picture to take home with her. Then her mama will show Lori which materials she can choose from. They are always the ones on sale. Then they will go to the baskets that have sale buttons and trims in them, and they'll choose things from there. Lori's mama always spends a lot of time sewing dresses, short sets, even pajamas for Lori, besides making her own dresses.

Lori's mama stands back and claps her hands in delight. "You are jus' the prettiest lil girl on earth! Now, tilt your head the way I showed you, and fold your hands in your lap so your shoulders are straight. Everyone wants to see that purty smile and those purty, pearly teeth. That's my girl, and now cross your feet at your ankles."

Lori dutifully does as her mama asks, while her mama smooths the fabric of the dress, adjusting the puffed sleeves, and the lace along the hem. Lori sees how mama loves the material, and asks her why she loves it so much. Lori loves the dainty flowers and the trims, but the cotton print feels all the same to her. Lori asks her mama why she always loves to run her hands on the material.

"Oh, child. If you'd ever had your mama dig through a stack of flour in bags looking for the prettiest sack, you'd know why. I get to dress my little girl up just like one of the dolls we see in those fancy stores. Everyone loves a pretty doll, and I am making sure everyone will love you the minute they set eyes on you, lil' darlin'."

Lori climbs off the chenille-covered iron bed and

goes over to the mirror on the bedroom door. She studies the reflection, from her little white shoes to her stiff curls. She tiltes her head and smiles at the reflection. Lori practices curtsying in the mirror. She tries her best to look like Shirley Temple. She wonders if Shirley's dresses has pretty colors like hers.

Lori listens to her mama talking to her about grades. Her mama tells her *while appearances and good manners will really help a girl, she still needed to get good grades so she could go on and go to college. The perfect woman is beautiful, cultured and smart, and that's what Lori will become one day when she is all grown up. Lori needs to go to college and she'll have to keep up good grades in high school to be able to go to college. Lori will need to win scholarships.*

But, Lori doesn't have a clue what she'd take in college. Her granddaddy told her not to worry about going to school. It was a waste of time and money. He told her to just choose a man with a lot of money to marry, telling her it is just as easy to love a rich man as a poor one. Lori knows her daddy's father resents their daughter-in-law having a college degree and what they consider *putting on airs*.

Lori's mama has gone back to work now that Lori is in junior high, and they have more money. Lori gets to have mostly store-bought clothes now, and they have meals that aren't cooked from scratch, too. Sometimes, they go out to eat, to restaurants that serve Italian or Chinese food. She heard her parents talking about buying new furniture, too.

Lori doesn't think she wants to be a teacher, like her mother suggested. She agrees with her daddy when he says teachers are a bunch of old biddies. None of them are pretty, or seem to be happy, either. Lori doesn't know what she wants to be, except always pretty and happy, even when she's that old. Maybe an ag. teacher wouldn't be so bad, but she's never heard of a woman teaching agriculture classes. And she doesn't think she could dress very nice since there were shop classes and would likely be trips to the school farm. Lori doesn't even want to picture manure splattered on high heels or dresses.

PART TWO

Chapter Seven

Me

I run the brush over my horse, hoping my dad will change his mind. The smell of the Old Gold cigarette clinched in his teeth is strong. I pick up a hoof and pull the hoof pick out of my back pocket. He watches me, and I am not sure why. Maybe to just get outside and get away from my mother.

I switch the wad of Copenhagen to the other side of my mouth, hoping he doesn't see it. He yelled at me last week about the chew, told me it made me act goofy. He said he asked some old friends who chew. That's how he knew it makes me goofy, but that's not the big issue today.

He won't allow me to rope. I can stack and haul hay, feed and halter-break my own FFA steer, and dig a ditch, but am not allowed to rope. He fears I may lose a finger, and *Lord knows it will be hard enough to marry me off*. If I lose a finger, no one will marry me. I bring up the fact that my girlfriends all rope, and he scowls and says that's because all their fathers are roping nuts. *Hell, they roped their own mothers' laying hens back in Oklahoma*. He is smug, because he came from Texas. He only knows hard-and-fast roping. Dallying scares him, although he lost three relatives to roping accidents back in Texas, because they were tied on.

Go figure.

He doesn't know that I chase and throw my rope at the yearlings in the irrigated pasture by the house when he and my mother are not home. I will try broaching the subject again tomorrow, maybe after supper, when he has drunk a couple of glasses of wine.

I dare not do what I did before about the steer/bull riding. After having the entry notarized, I checked the place next to girls' steer riding. It didn't go over really well, especially when I drew the only bull the contractor threw in the steer pen.

I am quiet, say my yes sirs, and put the horse away. It is Saturday night, and there is a dance in town. The little town with the small, white-painted churches with signs declaring that they are various types of Baptist, or

Methodist, or some other fundamental, protestant religion. The Catholic Church is the only one not painted white and sits on the edge of town.

Sprawling oaks and sycamore trees shade many of the homes with wisteria growing on the front porches. It could be a town in rural Oklahoma, Texas, Arkansas or even Missouri. That's because that's who built this town, folks from there. The VFW Hall will be hopping, the local band blaring honky-tonk music, while the constable and sheriff slowly drive by when they get bored watching the bar crowd a couple blocks away that includes a lot of our parents.

I have received my allowance and spend my money on cans of chew. A burger and a can of chew cost the same. I need to lose eight any way. My shoulders and thighs rival those of the football players.

I will be given the price of admission to the dance or Okie-stomp, as some of the kids call it. I am allowed to attend these dances because the VFW puts them on. The dollar and a quarter admission will also buy a bottle of Boone's Farm or T.J. Swan, and I can probably find a boy who will pay for my way into the dance. I sigh with relief. Finances are taken care of, and now my only other worry is that boy driving us to the dance picks me up first, or at least I am one of the first. That and hoping my folks don't see the bumper sticker. If any of us girls' parents knew how many kids were layered in the pickup, we wouldn't be allowed to go. The neighbor boy who has the ten-year-old pickup we crowd into charges each of us a quarter for gas, making a profit since gas is about thirty-five cents a gallon, and seven or eight of us will pay his fee.

My dark eyes are lined with heavy black liner, with little curly-q slashes at the corner of my eye, where squint lines will appear decades later. I have on cream-colored new boots. The toes are buck-stitched around the wing-tip of dark blue lizard skin, and I have chosen navy checked Wranglers to wear. My naturally dark brown short, pixie hair is dyed so black it is almost blue. This irritates my mother beyond measure. Folks are always calling me a throw-back, including my dad and my grandparents. Mom is a native Californian, all prim and proper. Her family, and some of the old antique furniture her family has, came around the Horn, and they think their crap doesn't stink. There are still tones of New York and back East in their mannerisms.

I am waiting to hear Tommy's pickup. I explain once again to my parents that he doesn't need to come in, and this is not a date. He just gives us rides since they won't let me drive. The driving is a real sore point. All the boys get to drive, and got to even before they had licenses. We girls cannot drive on a public road because we're girls, and that means we lack sense. We have bemoaned this until even we are sick of hearing it.

Next year, we will be old enough to have real, full-time licenses. Our parents think the farm licenses we have shouldn't be taken advantage of. The licenses are for when we absolutely have to get on pavement. But last weekend, I had to haul a trailer load of cattle thirty-five miles away on a winding mountain highway full of speeding log trucks. Guess that's different. Right?

Peggy

Peggy makes a face as she enters the utility room. She pulls her boots off, leaving the spurs on the boots, and sets them exactly in line next to her mom's. She unzips her jeans, and then unbuttons her shirt. "This is beyond ridiculous," she thinks. God forbid a single horsehair get in the house. The two poodles aren't a problem. Her mom doesn't think they shed. Peggy snorts at the thought. Her mother doesn't allow her to ride bareback, either. She has to totally undress and shower before she can come all the way into the house. Her mother did nothing but criticize her tonight in the arena as usual, when her dad isn't there. He is working late on his last job, building another custom-built house. He can never make enough money to make Peggy's mom, Sandy, happy. He loves to rope. Folks always said he was born with a rope in his hand. Lord knows the glassed-in wall in the living room holds enough of his buckles. Yes, her mom had some buckles and trophies from barrel racing and showing there, too. But, three quarters of the case are row after row of Mike's buckles.

Peggy unbraids her waist length dark hair and turns on the shower. She can't wait for the dance. It is a way to escape. She loves running the barrels and poles, tying goats, and is starting to really do well with her break-away roping. Her dad is proud of her, and she loves hearing him cheer her on. But she can never do well enough to please her mom, whether it is in school or in the arena. Her mom always acts like the family has to prove something. That they are as good, or even better than anyone else.

Her dad is home now and is warming up his horse when Peggy hears Tommy's loud truck start up the hill. She's come out to watch her dad after showering and primping, and is leaning on the fence.

"That your ride comin'?" Mike rode up and asks as he strokes the shiny mane of the horse he is riding.

"Yes, that's Tommy. He's giving Virginia a ride, too." Her dad likes Tommy. He works hard and is known among the adults as a good kid. Little do parents know. Tommy is good about working, real responsible, but he also really kicks up his heels, and has ways to get booze bought the rest of us don't have. She is hoping Tommy has removed the stupid bumper sticker that says, "*Save the West, Ball a Cowboy!*" or that he doesn't turn the truck around in front of her dad.

Peggy hurries to get into the truck with Tommy and me. She tells Tommy to turn right when he gets to the end of the drive. She explains her dad can see them from the arena, and knows they should be heading towards town, not towards the other kids' homes. It will mean taking the long way around to pick up Bobby.

I grab for the dash to keep from sliding into Peggy

as the loud truck makes the turn onto pavement. I explain our folks wouldn't let us go if they knew how many kids are gonna be piled in. For some reason, our parents don't think seven or eight kids in a 1960s pickup is a good idea.

We ate stacked two deep. Tommy finally pulls the truck into the dirt lot and parks under a large white oak, next to the irrigation district office. He whacks my knee with the gear shift in the process. I slug Tommy in the shoulder, and my elbow hits Peggy in the nose.

"Dammit, knock that crap off!" someone in the cab yells. It is impossible to tell who, though it is most likely from the bottom layer of kids. The doors open and we spill out, laughing and tucking shirttails into jeans that have hand carved belts with silver tips and keepers, and our names carved into the back of them.

Donna

Donna is there, in what passes for a parking lot, waiting for us girls to climb out. Lori, the rodeo queen slash cheerleader is with her. Gail stands quietly next to Donna. I inwardly groan at Lori being here. Those kinds of girls get on my nerves, no matter how long I've known them. A kid with his jeans half tucked into his boots is staggering around hollering, "I am a lover, fighter, and wild bull rider!" Geez, gonna be one of those nights.

"Hey, Donna," one of the boys says with a sly grin as he climbs out. She stares him down as his eyes travel to her chest. Short of wearing a t-shirt, Donna will always have cleavage. Her chest begins at her chin and ends at her waist.

"Glad you all came. My folks are at the bar, so they dropped us off," Donna says to me and Peggy. Donna looks around at the parking lot and asks the girls if anyone in the truck has any beer. Lori always acts so goody-two-shoes, and she will be the first to drain a wine bottle or a beer.

"Don't know; let's find out," I say with a grin. I nod to Donna, silently wondering what is worse, having Donna's chest, or having Virginia for a name. I blacked the last boy's eye who began calling me "Virginia the NON-VIRGIN-IA. Man, I wish my folks had gone with Georgia for my name, instead. I can handle the Ginny some of the kids call me, or even the V some of my family call me. Initials are always a big thing here for names. Shoot, my dad didn't even have a name until he went in the service for WWII. His folks only gave him initials. Dad's sergeant insisted he have a name, so Dad chose what he figured the initials stood for, one of his granddaddy's name.

The boys announce I can stop looking. They are going after beer. Tommy's brother will buy for them, like he does all the time. They hold their hats out to collect money. I ask if they'd please get a bottle of wine, and put on a worried face, as I say sadly that I only have enough for the wine, or to get into the dance. I sigh deeply and put on my saddest face.

The boys look away, fidgeting. Bobby finally says, "What kinda vino do you girls want? I'll get it, cuz I sure ain't going in and pay for the dance with you, spreading rumors that will hurt my reputation!" He winks at Lori, and I want to gag. I spit Copenhagen juice towards his boot, and he jumps. Peggy smiles sweetly and tells him what we want.

We girls head for the dance across the street. I follow Lori's steam-curled waves, caught up with a new big silver barrette. Suddenly she stops, and points to a van, a new one I'd not seen before.

"Have you seen Dusty's new van?" she asks coyly. "It is really cool, has a frig and stuff, besides a good bed." I want to ask how the bed feels. I bite my tongue.

She wants everyone to take the bait and ask how she knows what is inside of it. That girl just doesn't get it. Why does she make her reputation worse?

Chapter Eight

Donna and Me

The old hemp ropes look good, but man, are they a long way up there. I wish I could have put four ropes through the barrel, but I couldn't get a hole made to get a fourth rope strung through it. Donna and I decided a bucking barrel hung from the rafters in my folks huge one-hundred-year-old barn where there are years of old hay on the floor had a better chance of sliding by parents. When we tried to put one up using the trees, we were shot down in a hurry. My folks went to Reno this weekend, so we grabbed the opportunity to build this one while they were gone. Besides, I could just hear my granddaddy telling me to never pass an opportunity that the Good Lord just up and gave you.

Only problem is that three ropes make it want to roll. It really goes wild, beside the fact the rafters we threw the ropes over seem a mile high. We chose a barrel that already had two holes, and we were able to finally make another hole. No matter how hard we tried, we couldn't get a fourth hole made. So, the end with the bung hole only had one rope.

Donna wants to try the barrel first. We have already put an old bull rope on it, and tried pulling the long ropes to see how the barrel would buck. It looks like if we could ride this, we could ride anything with hair on it. None of our parents will allow us to even think about getting in a rough stock event, so we tell them a bucking barrel will help us with our horsemanship if any of our horses ever blow up. This is met with a parental eye roll. They don't know we had devised the best barrel ever for bettering our riding skills.

Donna jumps on the barrel, and I do my best to pull the old bull rope tight while the barrel just wants to roll sideways. I am secretly glad there is so much deep hay on the old floor. I doubt anyone will be able to stay on the rolling barrel.

I hear a loud truck pull in by the corrals and I bet it is Tommy with Bobby, one of the kids that tags along with him. His truck is loud and my dad told him he was shivering and shaking in bed when Tommy dropped me off after a dance. Dad told him he was pretty sure a rod was gonna come through the bedroom wall and get him while he lay in his own bed.

You have to just love parents. I guess being a teenager teaches you embarrassment, so when you have your own kids someday, you will know how to not turn red and want to die.

I hope he parks under the mulberry trees. The birds are loving those berries. Pink stained crap would make that old truck look better, I think with a grin. Donna and I look at each other, and she slides off the barrel. No way are we doing the test-run with them here. The big barn door creaks open, and the boys stand in the doorway. Sunlight shows the air is full of floating old hay, and they cough. There are two guys with Tommy. Bobby stands next to Tommy. Both of them are grinning. I think I've seen the other one. Maybe he is the new kid.

They look all cocky, pushing their hats back off red, acne prone faces and thinking they are so cool. They look at the barrel suspended from the high rafters and walk over to it. Tommy pulls hard on a rope, and the barrel tries to roll. He shakes his head and says we'll get killed. It is too wild, and no one will be able to ride it. He snorts and looks at us like we are dumb little kids. The three stooges look at each other and start laughing.

Donna glares at him, pulls the glove out of her back pocket, and starts to climb on the barrel. I have to go hold it, so she can get on. Oh man, she's gonna do the test run with them here. I pull the rope down while the boys watch. She wiggles up to her clenched fist, her bicep muscles popping out like Popeye. I see the boys eye it in surprise. She looks at me, and I step to where I hope I can reach all the ropes without getting smacked by the stupid barrel.

Donna sits back and sticks her massive chest out and nods. I begin pulling the ropes, hard as I can. We're gonna show these yahoos how a girl can ride. Donna is tipping forward, her dang chest is too big, throwing her off balance. I pull harder, the barrel is really going, in every direction, then one of the ropes breaks, singing through the air and smacks one of the stooges across the face, while Donna goes headfirst into one of the solid oak stanchions. Oh, man, she's probably dead! Broke her neck or her head open, or something awful. I start to run over, and the barrel loops through the air, knocking Tommy almost down as he runs to Donna. I dodge the crazy barrel and reach Donna first. She's rolled over and is slumped against the old wood. I can see her face is already swelling. Tommy pushes me out of the way and studies her face. He has her count his fingers and asks her the questions they always ask when you get hurt. I find a rag, run cold water over it, and hand it to her. I am not about to touch her; her lip is split, and I am wondering if her nose is broken. One eye is already so red and puffy that it looks like a golf ball is rising under her skin.

Tommy and the guys decide they should leave. They don't want to be anywhere close to this and have to deal with Donna's dad. I sit beside her, and tell her I can take her to the hospital, call my folks, call her folks, call the dang President, whatever she wants. She looks at me and laughs, while tears spring from her eyes. "Dang you, don't make me laugh. It hurts! You know we ain't calling anyone. I just need to sit still for a few minutes longer."

I am now afraid of broken ribs, despite their super-boob padding, and stare at her chest. "No, Dumbo, it hurt my face and head, not my chest!" I usually try to not even look that direction, especially since one of the tiny bull riders got drunk and said his biggest dream was to just jump up and down on Donna's chest, like a feather bed.

Donna begins to push herself up, and I stand and offer a hand to pull her up. She rests against the stanchions and looks a bit unsteady. We slowly make our way into the house, and I have her sit on the Naugahyde couch. I plan to go to get her a drink of water and ice for her head, and it makes me think of granddaddy again. He was always the one who did the doctoring. He always insisted a bottle of whiskey be kept at every camp or ranch for emergencies. Only problem was that it appeared that he had lots of emergencies. The last place my dad put Granny and Granddaddy on to take care of the cows had all the rafters above the porches filled with empty whiskey bottles. I reach up in the cupboard and pull a dusty bourbon bottle down. I grab a glass, throw some of the ice in, put the rest of the ice in a towel, and march out to her. I hand her the wad of towel and ice, then hand her the whiskey. I tell her to drink it, all of it, with as much authority as I can muster. She stares around the towel and tells me only if I do the same. I guess it is rude to not join her. After the first couple glasses, the whiskey went down a lot easier.

Both of us wake up with bad headaches the next morning. We find our clothes out by the corral, along with the empty whiskey bottle, and discover the ropes had all been cut on the bucking barrel. I guess we were pretty busy, but sure don't remember any of it. We roll the barrel into a dark corner, pull the ropes down, coil them, and hang them on a back wall. By that evening, we have a good story for our parents about how one of the ranch horses bucked Donna off for no good reason. Yep, that was why we had wanted a bucking barrel, but that's okay, we will just learn to ride the horses better without one. Yep, parents do know best. We will tell them that with straight faces.

Donna

Donna comes by and wants me up to ride into town with her. With her grandparents gone and her dad remarried, she gets to have a little looser rein. I need to get something for my folks at the post office, so my folks are glad they don't have to go into town. The air is hot and sticky, and we stop at the frosty, get cokes and dipped-top frosties, and watch the cars go by. When we've finished the ice cream, we drive down the old wide main street and see cop cars parked by the little park, where we've never yet seen a single soul use the park. The tiny park that boasts one bench under a giant cottonwood tree sits right next to the old yellow train depot building and the sign that explains how this little town came to be. The new post office building sits across the street. Donna and I both wonder why the constable and a county sheriff's car is there. We don't see any wrecked vehicles or even anything on the railroad track. Donna pulls into the side of the post office, and we see a bunch of folks have gathered and are staring at the park. We see the cops are looking at stuff on the ground.

"How are you boys today?" It is one of my dad's buddies. He thinks it is so funny to call all the girls boys. Especially when one of us is so obviously not a boy. He admires Donna's chest like every male I have ever known. I smile and say that we're fine before asking about what happened across the road.

"I'll tell you what happened, on account no one else is likely to. One of those hippies from San Francisco was hitchhiking his way to Oregon. Decided he was gonna get him a drink after walking past the auction yard. Came into the bar to tell us all how stupid we are, how the auction yard stinks, and we should be ashamed to have that in our town. Made fun of the God, Country, and Family sign, hanging there when you come into town, the one by the 4H, and the church listings sign. He got an offer for a ride. Outta of town. But not without stopping here first. The boys hogtied him and sheared his lousy long hair off with sheep shears right there in the park. They really didn't hurt him much, and if he'd have sat still, he wouldn't have gotten those nicks on his head. He doesn't know how lucky he was. There was talk of tar and feathers. We won't have that kind here. Now, the rest of them know it, and won't be trying to stop here. We are good, law abiding, God fearing folks, and we won't tolerate that kinda behavior."

I nod and go in to sign for the package. When I come back out, Donna is talking to someone else. She says her good byes, and we get in the car. "Holy moly!" Donna exclaims. We wonder if anyone we know was involved. I can sure see some of the fathers of the kids I know being part of it. I ask Donna if she heard what happened to the dude after they had the public sheep shearing of his hair.

She says they dumped him out by the creek near the freeway exit, still tied up. A new-to-town guy driving out there to fish saw him laid out there and took him on to the hospital, which is about twenty miles away. After talking to the shorn hippie, the new guy called the cops and wanted the shearing guys arrested. We both know that won't happen, and the picking up of the hair out of the grass is probably to destroy evidence anything ever happened rather than gather evidence.

Peggy

Peggy lives about a mile from me, and sometimes I ride down and use her arena. I don't like to, yet I do. All I have here at this place is a big corral, and some barrels set up in the pasture. It gets pretty hairy running barrels on the slick grass. My folks don't really like rodeos or horse shows. They're all about cows, and ranching. Mom's not about any of it, really, maybe just identifying wild flowers and grasses. She taught school and has a reputation for being a witch.

A couple of years ago I came home with the year-end trophy for the local gymkhana series. I'd ride my Dad's old ranch mare, a Hancock bred one, to the arena a few miles away, compete, and then ride home. They never even came to watch until I came home with the trophy, though Dad drove by to make sure I made it to the arena the first couple of times. The first time I ran in a single barrel event was so embarrassing. The old mare was fast, a ranch horse. We hauled butt down to that barrel, and she threw the brakes on, sliding straight to the barrel rather than around it, and tried to stick her head in it, trying to figure out why there wasn't grain in that barrel. We taught each other a lot going to those deals. I only had plain ranch style tack, really it was Texas style. I didn't have any fancy silver, braided reins and romal, or any of the other fancy California-style stuff. Heck, I didn't even have the stuff they used for rodeo, like roping reins and tie-downs. I finally got a good horse a couple years later when my folks figured out I wasn't going to quit doing it and that I was pretty darn good at it.

Peggy's mom has come out to watch us ride. Peggy looks and acts nothing like her mom, Peggy is average size and a brunette with kinda hawk-like features, the nice way of saying the Indian/Okie shows in her breeding. She has the cheekbones that are really high with what is politely called a prominent nose. Peggy's mom is petite, platinum blonde from a bottle, and freckled. Peggy's mom always puts on airs, like she is something special. When Peggy and I pull up to let the horses breathe after a few laps around the arena, Sandy's eyes bore holes in my tack and horse, checking out every detail. The questioning begins.

"Do your folks still have the foot hill ranch? That runs a lot of cows, doesn't it? How about the place your grandparents were on? Do they still have that, too?"

I swallow hard, grateful my folks aren't here. Everybody, and I mean everybody, knows you don't ask, or even hint at asking about how many cows someone owns. I try to figure how to answer before I reply. She's hinting, without flat-out asking things that she knows she shouldn't. Probably figuring I am a dumb kid who will tell her. If she knew my folks very well, she'd know better. Business is something never discussed outside our home, period. Daddy had sold one of the ranches, the one I grew up on, and bought investment property to make my mother happy. Mom was the only one happy.

I try to smile, and tell her nope, that it is being sold. Which it is. Despite it breaking my heart. Mom made Dad do it. She's always hated ranching. Dad has bought some investment properties, a bunch of rentals. Oh, I'm sure happier than a hog in corn for that, I think bitterly. I am not about to tell Miss Busy-Body Sandy a damn thing. Despite getting razzed by everyone for being from what they call "up in the rocks," I'd give about anything to be back at that place with the rocked-in-spring by the old house. There's no electricity up there. There is a phone with a party line. You can hear someone on it a lot of the time, thinking they are being silent, but their breathing will give them away. Sometimes, they can only stand it so long before they have to throw their two cents worth into the conversation. I'd still rather be with those folks in that rough lava rock strewn country than some of the folks down here, thinking they are real cowboys when they are nothing but Rexall Rangers.

Me

The ag teacher does his usual thing, talking in a monotone until we're about asleep, then roars like a fire and brimstone preacher, making everyone almost jump out of their seats. Mr. Jackson calls on me, knowing I will give the correct answer. I answer correctly, even when he probes deeper. He almost smiles. I am his pet. Mr. Jackson is tall and rangy, and not someone you mess with. He is real strict. I got caught forging his signature last week, and he didn't tell the principal. He actually told him he likely wrote the pass. He doesn't care if there's chew in his class, as long as no one spits. You can spit when you are on a team and are traveling in a school car on a way to competition. Being well mannered around adults almost always pays off, I discovered.

I win the state livestock judging at both big colleges last month, bringing the trophies back to our high school. He drug me into Parli-Pro. I really had no choice. You don't tell Mr. Jackson no. He simply announced I had a good vocabulary and was on the team. My folks laughed when I went home and told them. I don't do public things, things that call for a person to stand still and talk in front of a bunch of people. I used to hide in a closet or under the bed when visitors came, even when it was cousins or aunts or uncles. Shoot, most folks thought I couldn't even talk 'til I went to school.

He asks what I was going to have for a project, and I said I wasn't. My folks dodn't want to loan me any money. He takes me to the bank, and gets me an FFA loan. Takes me to the ranch with the best club calves, and we chose what he thinks will be the grand champion. My dad always looks down his nose at Mr. Jackson, saying how Mr. Jackson's daddy was never any account, and that he only worked for other folks his whole life. I love Mr. Jackson. He believes in me, and always stands up for me.

Mr. Jackson goes to the chalkboard and begins drawing on it, explaining about reproduction in cattle. This is the closest we will ever get to sex-ed, besides the girls fifth grade class about puberty, sanitary napkins, and using deodorant. When he turns around, he sees Marion messing around in the back of the room. The big eraser is thrown so fast that it is a blur. Marion jumps up, holding his head, beginning to blubber. Like having Marion for a name isn't bad enough, he is actually gonna cry in front of everyone. I've only cried in public once, and it sure wasn't over being whapped by an eraser on account I was fooling around.

Mr. Jackson strides down the aisle and looks down at Marion. Marion stops blubbering and asks to be excused. He is told that he is excused, for the semester. To not come back. Marion is such a spaz.

I stay for the next class. I will be in the ag office

between the classroom and the shop the two ag teachers share. I am their assistant, grading papers, making copies, and helping to set up lesson plans. I hear hollering from the shop side, and carefully peek through the blinds. Girls can't take any shop classes, though I hope we will be able to in a couple of years. Heck, since they opened FFA up to girls, we have made the organization so much better, and there are a ton of girl officers like me. Anyway, Mr. Jackson had gotten angry the day before when half his shop students were so busy talking about an upcoming rodeo that he yelled at them. He told them "not a damn one of 'em could ride a stick horse". The boys all made stick horses, and now they were galloping around on them. He is hollering at them about what gunsals, what Rexall Rangers, they are. I quickly drop the shade and bend over my papers before the door opened. He starts chuckling as soon as he steps in, saying to himself the boys had sure got him good. I pretend to not hear. I know he has forgotten that I am there.

Lori

Lori batts her mascared-to-death eyelashes. I want to giggle. The black smudges around her eyes get larger with each flutter. I am not about to tell her, either. We have run into the big barn at the college, out of the heavy January rain. Our blue corduroy FFA jackets are soaked. She makes a point of doing a little slithering shiver as she moves closer to the judge. She really thinks one of the livestock judges is going to fall for a high school student. I don't tell her she looks like a raccoon instead of a Maybelline advertisement.

Granddaddy always said you have an eye for livestock, or you don't. I think he is right, Lori doesn't have a clue, and is always trying to cheat and read my sheet for judging. The rain lets up enough for us to make our way to the Student Union for lunch. We can see it is crowded, and just as I begin to pull the big doors open, we hear screams, see people jumping up and chairs falling over. Lori crowds past me into the building, and a running naked man slams into her. Streaker! Wow! *They really do that* is my first thought. I see Lori all red-faced and flustered, and ask snidely under my breath why she can't keep hold of him. One of the judges comes up to make sure we are okay, and Lori manages to let out a half credible sob and falls into his arms. Lord, take me now! I can't believe even she would go to this length. The judge looks over her now limp hairdo at me. I shake my head, full of disgust. I know dang well she will be savoring the story of the handsome judge being so concerned about her in a matter of hours.

I now stand in the college dean's office, staring out the window. Mr. Jackson sent me in here to give my account of the streaking incident. He will have enough problems when we get back to our school with parents accusing him of being irresponsible and allowing this to happen on a field trip. The same parents who raise heck with the radio stations because Conway and Tanya are singing about sex, yet are honky-tonky fools on Saturday night, and send their children to one of the white churches on Sunday mornings. This whole town is nothing but a country song, come to think of it. Too many lyrics ringing true are filling my head.

After being released from the Dean's office, I board the bus with the rest of the students. I see Lori in the back giggling and playing grab-ass with a couple of the boys. Her makeup has been repaired, and she has unbuttoned the white regulation blouse far enough to give the boys a peek. So much for her being trauma-tized.

Mr. Jackson stands in the front of the bus, and asks if everyone is on, then announces our chapter has done very well, even the gunsal stick horse riders with their welding contests and I am at the top for all four classes of livestock judging, either first place or tied for first.

He slides into the seat in front of me, and tells me quietly that I am up for the State Ag. Student Award, which will mean a full-ride scholarship to Cal-Poly. I smile and slowly digest the information, wondering what my folks will say.

Gail

Gail is with Donna when they pull up to the barn. They get out in their cut-off jean shorts and halter tops. Donna is the one in a halter top. Why? I think it makes her look bigger than ever, but maybe it is cooler. I don't know, I don't have that trouble. Anyway, I continue brushing my FFA steer. I realize Goober is becoming cow-hocked, and make a mental note I need to walk him more. It will be good to lead him while I am making wet blankets on my mare. I have washed and am now brushing and curling the Hereford steer. I am hoping to train his hair to curl, hoping I have better luck with his than I have with my own hair. I am trying some new gel, the Dippidy-do stuff just doesn't work. I will add hair spray afterward and see if that will help. An old man who has registered cattle told me he waters down white glue and uses that on his cattle. I am not ready to try that on my own hair yet. I do know some old ladies who dilute boxed jello in their favorite colors to use for hair gel. I thought showing horses was bad. Granny always tells me you can't curl a cow's tail when referring to my hair. I gave up and have a super short haircut, like Liza Minnelli, a pixie it is called. I have to tape the peaked cut sides to my cheeks at night.

I call Gail over, and they come, slipping between the corral rails. It takes Donna a couple times to find a place where she can get through. Gail lights a cigarette and starts in about the new guy and how stupid her boyfriend is for just leaving her all alone on the weekends, especially with his pickup so she can haul her own horses to the shows. She blows a smoke ring and laughs about picking up the new guy and making out with him in her boyfriend's truck. I frown at the cigarette and tell her it is a good thing my folks are not home and that there isn't any hay close, adding a choking cough to emphasis my dislike of the smoke. I lock eyes with Donna, who looks away, finally. I think what a slime ball Gail is, and a picture pops into my head.

"Gail, you ever see anything like this?" I ask her and she comes up to Goober real fast. He just stares at her, he's gotten really tame. Gail peers at my hand lying on his back. I know full well Gail has never fed-out an animal for the fair. I should be up for an acting award. This is gonna be great.

"He's got this weird knot; do you think it feels like those cysts the horses get?" I ask innocently.

She peers down closer to look at it as I begin massaging the bump. I talk about how it kind of rolls around under the skin and how weird it is and urge her to look really close to see if it has a hole in it. As her face gets within inches, I squeeze the bump, hard. The skin pops open and the warble larvae spews out, splattering her, and I am falling over laughing. The slime is on her face and even her lip. Donna starts to laugh, and I fear her halter-top may not be up to the challenge. She bites her lip when Gail starts screaming and her eyes fill with angry tears while muttering halfheartedly about that being a chicken-crap thing to do. Goober, the steer, is getting wide-eyed at the loud laughing and Lori's screams. He steps on my foot, and doesn't want to get off. Okay, Goober, I get it. Payback ain't much fun, especially when even the animal doesn't approve.

Chapter Nine

Me

It is the last gymkhana show of the season for the local riding club. The dust is fine and it is still hot in late September. I wonder where the water truck is. The dust is stirred and lifted by the slightest of breezes. We can wear short sleeves to this deal. They do require hats, so I have on a Larry Mahan shaped straw, as does Peggy. Donna and Gail have on candy straws, matching their blouses. I hate those plastic colored hats, you can't shape them and they are uncomfortable. They also look like they are made of Rainbow or Wonder bread wrappers all woven up. Donna has entered these things forever, along with Gail. They are into the horse shows and parades a lot more than me. There's not really a lot I like about horse shows, and the one-piece polyester material you show in is another reason. Talk about uncomfortable.

Sometimes Lori comes now that she's the local rodeo queen, if she figures there's a chance to wear her dumb tiara and sash. She's not here being Her Highness today. Peggy and I attend when we don't have anything better to do. It is good for our horses, and adds to our ribbon and trophy collection. Peggy is way ahead of me on the ribbons, and has a quilt made of them. This arena is where I went for my very first horse show/gymkhana. Man, what I have learned since then.

Most of the parents have backed their pickups up to the arena fence. They're sitting in the beds or beside the truck in lawn chairs, some of them are drinking beer out of Styrofoam ice chests and being loud. The drunker they get, the louder they get. They start going up and entering friends in things like the barrel crawl, egg race and other silly stuff. It is pretty funny to watch some of the fat old men try to jump off and crawl through the barrel. One-time old Waylon, Gail's daddy, got stuck in the barrel. We girls laughed our butts off.

The adults who are here and serious about the deal stay away from this side of the arena, sitting instead in the stands or by their trailers. They ignore this bunch for the most part, only occasionally sending dirty looks in our direction. I honestly have never figured out which side is worse, the snobs or the hicks.

I make a good barrel run, and am waiting for the stake race. I decide to go enter a couple more events since I'm having a decent day, and get a coke. I jump off without using my stirrups to look cool and tie my horse to the fence. I remember I need more rubber bands for my stirrups, anyway. I lost one during my last run. Some of the hoo-rawing crowd spot me and wave me over.

"Good run, girl! Bless your heart, that little ol' horse shore can run!"

I smile and say thanks, and look toward the concession stand. One of the older guys, he's probably forty, motions me closer and drops his voice down low. I feel like I could just stand there and get drunk off his breath. Jeepers creepers, talk about beer breath.

"Are ya'll heading that way? Would you do me a favor and take this for me? Enter ol' Billy up in the goat tying, will you?" he whispers hoarsely. He presses some damp bills he's pulled out of his front jean pocket into my hand. Yuck. I'm hoping the damp is from sweat or spilled beer. I have to smile and tell him yes-sir. Boy, isn't Lori gonna love this. Her ol' dad riding her horse, and gonna try to tie a goat. I smile as sweet as I am able and say I'd be proud to do it.

I get my coke and do as I was told, handing the rolled-up wad of money to the woman taking entries. She shakes her head and tries to suppress a smile as she writes it down. I try to not laugh, she finally snorts, and we both break out laughing.

My good deed is done, respecting my elders and following their orders, I think smugly. I saunter over to the fence. I see someone has brought the goat in and it is tied at the far end of the arena. It is bellaring obnoxiously, probably the first time for it to be in the arena. Or maybe not. Maybe it knows what's coming. Goat tying isn't something I like to do. They smell, they scream and holler like you are killing them and it doesn't take much to make 'em piss.

I lean back and let the ice-cold coke run down my throat. I think chewing makes my throat and mouth dry. I sure do get thirsty, and it keeps me occupied and slows my automatic firing mouth that gets me into trouble. And I can take a chew instead of eating, it has helped a lot with dieting. When I lower my head, I see Lori's dad Billy is riding in, but not on Lori's horse. This is an appy, big ol' Roman nose and blanketed with a ton of spots, prancing sideways. The tie down is as tight as my daddy and the appy's eye is rolling. I can tell by the set of Billy's hat he is half crocked. His overly-large body is slanted to one side in the saddle, one pant leg is caught in the top of his Justin ropers. This has *wreck about to happen* written all over it.

When the flag drops, he spurs the horse and grabs the horn, barreling down to the goat. I wonder if he sees the flag with one eye or both. Good Lord. He pulls up when he figures in line with the goat and jumps off. I am thinking double vision is a real issue at this point. Billy is a calf roper, and a team roper. Lately, mostly a team roper. He's gotten too big and too round to get off like he used to. And the booze makes his hands fumble. Billy trips and falls, face first. I try not to laugh out loud. I bite my lip to control myself, then switch my chew around. While I am trying to not cry from holding big hiccupping guffs of laughter in, I hear the crowd sounding alarmed.

I manage to see through my tears that the horse is running after the goat, the horse's stout neck bent to bite and occasionally striking at the goat. Wow, a goat hating horse. Who knew? Oh, crap! Billy has managed to get to his knees and waves his hat to the crowd that he is sure is worried about him. He gradually makes it the rest of the way up, dusts his pants off and replaces his now bent Panama straw on his round pumpkin head. He smiles and waves at the crowd again before noticing the horse is chasing the screaming goat who is screaming like only a goat can scream. He begins to roll in a forward motion toward the goat and horse, (he's too fat to run) hollering at the horse. The horse slows and looks down his big old nose at Billy. The goat sees what it figures is a chance and runs back the other direction. Drunk Billy is now swearing at the horse, and waving his short arms. When Billy finally makes it to within a few feet of the wide-eyed horse, the horse decides it should run. Billy has informed it he knows his full pedigree is not on his papers. At least not on the dame's side. The horse has been effectively hobbled by the goat's tie rope and slowly falls down, narrowly missing Billy. The goat screams again as it is jerked by the fall of the horse. I am dying, this is too funny. I see some men have jumped the fence and have freed the goat and helped Billy sort the mess out. Bless their hearts.

I can't wait to see Lori's face in class. I know I won't even have to mention the incident, someone, probably several people, will beat me to it. Come to think of it, I know I'll hear all about it at Chew Corner at school on Monday morning.

Me and Suzy

The heat and humidity from all the animals stifles me. I lay back on a bale of hay and stare at my fat steer I am sharing a stall with. I almost wish I could wash him again, at least the water will feel good. Someone said some of the sheep had really gotten sick, and one or two died from the heat. Why they have the District Fair in the hottest part of the summer is beyond me. Heck, the courthouse thermometer showed 120 degrees in the stinkin' shade yesterday, and with the lawn sprinklers going, too. Dad told Granny it is hotter than a popcorn fart. It is just too hot to do much of anything.

I see Suzy headed this way with her boyfriend, they're holding hands and she's giggling. She has on powder blue Wrangler cut-offs and a flowered print peasant top of the same color. Her leg muscles are deeply defined with every step, and her shoulders and arms are rounded and solid. Her waist is probably eighteen inches, I think with disgust. I hate having a twenty-four-inch waist, and big ol' thighs and shoulders. She's one gal no one wants to mess with. She's really short, has to be, to flip around those horses doing all those tricks. Folks don't think about how much strength it takes to pull yourself up with one arm or leg, especially on a running horse. A taller girl would bust her head open hanging off a horse like that.

Rumor is that her boyfriend does drugs. That's why

he is always winning all the rough stock events. Some guys say he snorts cocaine right before he climbs in the chute. He's so high, he thinks he's invincible. He's cute, but a real flirt. Big brown eyes like a deer, and as muscular as she is. They could have muscle babies, I think with a giggle. I don't trust him as far as I could throw him. He's worse than a woman, batting those long black lashes. Suzy steers him towards me and stops at my stall and asks if I am gonna be around. They're wanting to go swimming, and she wants to know if I will feed her steer this evening for her if they don't get back. She winks at me and says they might get lost on that big ol' lake after dark and not make it back. I reluctantly agree after getting the information on his rations. I ain't shoveling any of his crap, though, I got news for her. I may need a favor sometime, anyway. Never hurts to have someone owing you a favor.

I decide to do my own stall cleaning before I hit the shower. The midway has some new rides I want to try. I am hoping someone will be around to ride with. I just wish the dang carnies didn't have to always pick me out to holler at. I am not skilled at any of those dumb games. Last year a bull rider and I set the record for riding the Hammer twenty times straight, without getting off. I don't scream and act like some girly-girl, and I love to ride the scariest ones. I just have to make sure I have on clothes that stay put. Halter tops can come untied on some of these rides, depending on who is in the seat behind you.

Just as I am coming out of the shower, I see Suzy's folks. They're looking at the manure piled up behind her steer, and talking to each other. I hope they notice he is actually eating, that he has been fed and his water tub is full. I don't want to go over there, so I quickly dump my dirty clothes on top of the brushes and the Orvus jar in my show box and head for the midway.

I get in line for a corn dog, realizing I am hungry. I have on a short shirt, gathered neck style that leaves my midriff bare and regular blue Wranglers. My latest belt buckle is big and I'm glad it covers my belly button. I am wishing I had put something longer on for a shirt. The elastic in the bottom of the shirt makes me feel like the whole deal could go popping up over my bra. The guy that I rode all the rides with last year comes up behind me, squeezing me around the waist. I recognize that cologne. I hope my fat roll hiding under my buck-stitched belt with the trophy buckle doesn't come sliding out. I suck my breath in hard.

"Hey, gal! Ready to ride?" he asks. He is just a flirt. He does this with every girl. He is cute, always has starched shirts, jeans with the creases pressed and smells so dang good. 'Course, none of us girls seem to mind the flirting.

I grin in answer to his wink, cover the corn dog with mustard and share the big coke with him as we head for the midway. I know some mouths will be wagging about us, he has hooked a finger in my belt loop and we're giggling, sharing the coke while we stroll along the carnival booths. He wins me a big ol' teddy bear in answer to the carnies hollering at him he needs to get me something.

Chapter Ten

Lori

The music booms and the old wooden dance floor bends with the beat. I head for the front door to get some air, squeezing past the guys hanging in the hallway. Why they hang by the restrooms is beyond me. I hear some exclamations and some swear words in shocked tones as I finally get close to the wide-open doors. I see a bloody-face girl being helped along into the restroom by a couple of older girls. I recognize Lori's stiff curled hair and see the blood is slowly following the spirals of those curls, dripping off the ends.

Crap! I turn on my heel and follow the procession

into the door marked Fillies. I stare and listen to her yelling at the older girls to not call her folks, to call her cousin instead. I remember Lori lost an older cousin a few years ago in a car wreck. I get bits and pieces of the story by just watching and listening. Lori was with the new boyfriend, the new very drunk boyfriend. They'd gone to make a beer run, and were on their way back to the dance, only a few blocks away. They hit a parked car. A big ol' Cadillac. She remembers looking down at the speedometer when he yelled "We're gonna show that SOB about stopping in the middle of the road!" The speedometer read 90 when she looked over at it. When she looked up she saw the car's tail lights before the rear-view mirror hit her head, and the motor came crashing through, hitting her legs.

He told her if she could go, to run to the dance and get help, but to get away fast no matter what so she wouldn't get in trouble. What he should have said was for her to run so he didn't get in trouble. He was twenty-one with an underage girl. She said she began to run, stumbling and wiping the warm blood out of her eyes. When she arrived at the dance out of breath and dazed she was still holding the broken, bloody mirror she had pulled out of her forehead. I saw big splinters of glass around one eye, and in the middle of her forehead. One of the girls ask if I knew Lori's cousin's phone number. I shake my head, but said she'd be in the phone book hanging by the pay phone in the hall.

I slowly go up and gently get ahold of her hand while one of the gals goes to the pay phone. Someone has some change in their boot, something our mothers always make sure we carry. That way, we have money to call home if we need to. We get Lori to sit down in the stall, afraid to take her outside in case of the cops see her. I stare at the bloody floor and get a wad of towels to wipe it up. Hopefully, enough boots have wiped out the trail she had to have left in the hall.

Lori's cousin and husband arrived, and ask us all what happened. We all say we dodn't know, she has shown up like this. While I don't like the new guy, I'm not about to tell on anyone. Lori can tell them what she wants. I'm not about to get involved beyond being there for Lori if she needs me. While Lori drives me crazy most of the time, she is still a friend.

Lori comes to school on Monday and sits by me on one of the benches at Chew Corner. Some stupid jock with blond curls and his letterman jacket comes by and says he's never seen a Francis-stein before, particularly a Francis-stein goat-roper-cheerleader, laughing as he walks away. I spit at him, leaving a nice big tobacco stain on the back of his Levi jeans. He doesn't know I did it, and we laugh at him. It is good to see Lori laugh. She says it hurts to laugh, though. Pulls all those scabbing up places on her face.

I really look at Lori for the first time since Saturday night. She is missing half of an eyebrow and most of the skin on her cheekbone is scraped off. Her forehead is marked with slashes and stitches. She reminds me of the old photo my Dad keeps hidden of my Indian great grandmother. She had tattoos or something like that across her forehead. Lori is blond and blue-eyed, but the mess on her face is similar.

Lori says she decided cheer leading is not for her any longer. Especially after the letterman and the rest of the team started calling her Frances-stein, too. The other cheerleaders treat her like she is a leper, acting like looking at her face makes them sick. She confides that she knows who her real friends are now. She just hopes her face will heal right. The new boyfriend dropped out of her life and moved away, mostly on account of the town constable's suggestion.

She is relying on us girls and her friend and cousin Tommy to help her get her head back on straight, though none of us girls know it. The thought we can help someone like that would never have occurred to us. On the other hand, Tommy always tries to take care of everybody.

Peggy and Me

Peggy and I decide we really need to go to the next town to check out their western store and see some new faces, mostly new foxy guy faces, we're thinking. We slowly drive down the extra wide main street of our little town, past the false front buildings sitting a few feet higher than the road. Iron rings for tying up teams are still set into the sidewalk. The whole main street is set up so big teams and wagons could turn around without problems and then be tied in front of the old buildings. Sometimes I wish I lived in those days. Then I think about dragging around in a long dress and petticoats with no kind of air conditioning, and cooking on a wood stove when it is 110 degrees or higher. Nope, that's not for me.

Peggy's dad lets us take their new dually and we're careful to wave at folks we know and act like good kids. She turns the blinker on at the end of the main street and we go under the trestle that someone has spray painted JESUS LOVES THE HAYBUCKERS!

She looks in the rear-view mirror, then turns and grins at me. She stomps the gas pedal and we both say, "Let them ponies run!"

Peggy tells me her mom tried to stop her from getting to go. Peggy got an A- on her report card. I don't want to bad-mouth her mom, so I just work my chew around. In some ways, Peggy is lucky. She has better stuff than I do, despite my dad having more money than most folks. That whole Dust Bowl thing has made him tighter than anyone I know, even than my grandparents. Granddaddy even told Dad he'll crawl through a window to save the hinges on a door.

We merge onto the new freeway that cuts through rolling hills dotted with oak trees and Hereford cattle. The next town sits on the river, and is just another old town, but quite a bit bigger. They have a big junior rodeo, a punkin roller rodeo and a Pro Rodeo. They also have a bit more farming, especially to the south.

Peggy parks the big apple-red dually on the street in front of the saddlery, where a life-size plastic bay horse is mounted on the second story. Some guys waiting for the signal to change whistle at us as we climb out of the truck. We giggle and act like they don't exist. Century old brick buildings line the street and the saddlery sits on the corner. I love the smell of leather that greets us when we push the old door open. The tinkling bell tied on the door announces our arrival. I go to check out the silver case while Peggy talks to the saddle maker in the back. He ropes with her dad, and he asks how she's been doing. We both end up with a new color of checked jeans and leave drool marks on the silver case. There's some jewelry that will match Peggy's big silver barrette with the horse head in the center. I see a silver filigree tip and keeper I want for my new belt. We'll come back, I know.

We climb back into the truck and Peggy sees the whistlers walking on the sidewalk behind us. They whistle again, and pull their hats off, bowing to us and waving their arms. Peggy is flustered, and shoves the truck into reverse, popping the clutch, and turns to look over her shoulder to back up. The boys are getting closer, and she gases the big truck. The crunch we hear stops us dead. Crap. We look at each other, knowing this is in no way a good thing. The guys are shaking their heads, standing outside my window on the sidewalk. We slowly get out to see a tiny sports car that now has a big dent in its shiny hood where the trailer hitch pushed it in. No way could Peggy see it there, it was too short and too small. The guys grin and say they were trying to tell us it was there, but we just ignored them. Sure, they were.

The folks from the saddle shop and adjoining businesses come out. The saddle maker shakes his head, and tells us to come in and call Peggy's folks. He cocks his head and says, "I know ya'll couldn't see that little squirt of a car. Hurry up, I hear a si-reen already."

Peggy is on the phone when the young deputy comes to question us. His white Stetson and shiny boots, make him look like a Texas Ranger. He winks at me and says to relax. I tell him the driver is on the phone with her folks. Lord, I feel bad for Peggy, I can just imagine hearing Sandy now.

Chapter Eleven

Me

Fireworks shoot above the big ol' pine trees around the arena. Fourth of July in the cool mountains. This rodeo always draws folks wanting to escape the valley heat. The mountain hillbillies in charge are gonna run some timed events first I see, after watching a single barrel being unloaded near the end of the arena. The bucking chutes are empty. I wonder if any of them bothered to look at their program or even know the order of events. Most likely not.

Tommy asked me earlier if I would enter the rescue race with him. I hope it isn't the first event, and I'm betting the hide race will be first. I did that last year, and for the last time. Man, did I biff it. The hide rolled with me, and the rope got caught under the horse when we turned the barrel. It was just flat out ugly. So was I when it was over. I had dirt up my nose, down my pants and in my boots. My shirt lost some of the pretty pink snaps. Not a good place for a pink flowered blouse and white Wranglers. I won't be doing that again.

I jump off the fence and head for my horse. The night will get cool up here, unlike the valley. A jacket is a good idea for later. I hear voices by the trailer and see a couple of kids who live up here standing by my trailer. They're passing a Mason jar back and forth.

"Hey, gal, wanta try some shine? My granddaddy makes the best there is." The boys giggle and I can see them swaying.

"No thanks, I'm good." I hope they go somewhere else, I don't want them drunk and by my horse. One year a kid got so drunk up here on moonshine his buddies put him in a stock trailer, the kind with wide spaced rails. He was so messed up he couldn't figure out how to get out. He hollered and yelled half the night for someone to let him out. Too drunk to reach thru the bars and undo the latch. That's way drunk.

I grab a goose down coat before I ride away to warm up. Tommy's family is camped up here. I hear his grandmother's Arkansas twang. She's calling the dog she named Sofilthy. It is some kind of a white curly poodle cross. I grin as I weave between the trailers to get to the warm up area. Thank God, my folks are staying in town at a motel. There's enough parents around for everyone.

Tommy comes up as I trot my horse around. He says he has bull riding right after the rescue race, so he is hoping we're up early. He says the girls' steer riding is supposed to come later, but who knows with the way they run things. I nod and resume trotting. This isn't a rodeo put on by the valley contractor, so Tommy has no say in anything. He stands watching me, hands on his thin hips. He has on his gray grizzly, guess he figures a felt hat is okay in July since we're in the mountains. He should know better. Now, he is gonna try and give me directions like I don't know anything. At least I know better than to wear a hairy felt hat in July.

"Don't be afraid to haul ass and turn that barrel, I will get up there."

"Don't you worry, you better just hold on." I love giving him a hard time.

"You want me to help you get on your steer? I'll pull your rope for you." Now he's trying to be nice. I waited until my folks had signed and had the entry notarized before checking the box next to the girl's steer riding event. The usual events had all been marked, poles, barrels, ribbon race, etc. I know I'll be in trouble, my folks won't even know until they call my name. I really don't care much about bull riding. I want to ride bareback broncs, but they don't offer bareback broncs to girls in junior rodeos. I figure getting on any kind of rough stock will help me. At least until I can get a chance to get on a bareback bronc.

The announcer is finally in the stand, rattling off sponsors and the usual stuff. I hear chutes rattle below him. Then he announces the girls' steer riding will be the first event, right after the National Anthem. Oh, boy, my stomach turns a bit and I decide I better put my horse behind the chute side of the arena out of sight. I don't want my folks wondering why I'm not on my horse.

I look the steers over that are waiting to be loaded into the bucking chutes. They don't look too bad, mostly like roping steers. They're pretty much like railroad ties with heads and horns and thin tails. Pretty bony and narrow to ride, I am thinking. I go behind the chutes where Tommy and Bobby are waiting. Tommy starts acting all bossy and tells me I'm in the last chute. We walk over and he looks at the yellow hued steer and bends down and looks again. "That's a damn bull," he says to no one in particular. The man on the catwalk looks down at him and says they ran out of steers, so they had to throw a little bull in. Bobby stares up at me. I try to not look alarmed, try to look like I am as cool as Paul Newman in Cool Hand Luke.

But, dang it. My luck to get the only stinking bull in the bunch. Some of the other guys I know crowd around the chute while I climb over and get settled. One of the dumbos asks if I want him to slap my face. Another asks if I got all warmed up. They are acting like the spazzes they are, spurring the air and making God-awful faces. I dread the moment they call my name, knowing my folks are going to be furious. I'm not sure what is worse, getting on this bull or facing my folks afterward. I just hope they don't cause a scene and try to stop the rodeo.

The gate swings open, the bull jumps out, and I am thrown forward. I try to get back in position, but it is too late. He bucks again, and I go over his head. At least I cleared his horns, I think, as the ground comes rising at an alarming speed. I feel his hoof when it steps on my arm. I jump up fast, not wanting to scare my folks. The longest three seconds in my life just passed. It feels like three hours.

The clown guides me back to the fence, and I am hiding the fact my arm is killing me. Once I get through the gate and behind the chutes I plop down. I feel nauseated, maybe both from the ride and the pain in my arm. Tommy comes up and sees me holding my arm and demands to see it. After giving up on arguing, I carefully roll my sleeve up and see the abrasion where the bull stepped on it. The elbow area is swelling rapidly. Tommy sends me over to the ambulance to have them look at it. The two women and one man cluck over it and tell me I need to go have x-rays. I tell them I can't go to the doctor or hospital right now. I ask if they can they just splint it until I can go. They finally agree, pack some ice on it and let me go. I gingerly work the rolled-up sleeve down. I can just get my sleeve over the wrapping.

My arm is hidden under the long sleeve, but, it is sure throbbing. I will stay away from my parents as long as possible. The last thing I want to hear is I'd better not be hurt, and that I am probably grounded. I manage to tighten the cinch on my horse and climb on. I realize I can't use my arm and kinda plop in the saddle. My horse turns around and looks at me, wanting to know what the heck is going on. The Rescue race is next and I can't wimp out from riding in it. That would be a sure way for my folks to know I am hurt.

I wait my turn quietly at the gate. I am one of the lucky ones. My mare isn't the typical flighty, ding-a-ling, barrel horse. She'll always stand quiet. We can ride in and line up and she doesn't get all stupid and start prancing around or rearing or worse. We walk in the arena and see Tommy take his place by the barrel at the far end. I line up my horse, make sure she sees where we are headed, and we haul butt. My splinted arm is out straight in front of me and holding onto the horn to keep it from getting hurt any further. Tommy looks surprised at the speed we're sliding into the barrel. I barely slow and look down for him to jump on. I kick my boot free from the stirrup for him to use. He thinks he's so good, let's see him make this jump, I think with a wicked grin. He throws his foot in the stirrup and grabs for something to help him get behind my saddle. That something was my splinted arm. He cusses me loudly, telling me to whoa-up. I can feel myself blanch as he pulls himself up, and behind me, using my splinted arm. The wooden splint breaks, making a loud sound like a shot. I swear like a sailor, or a sawmill worker, as one of my friend's daddy said later. The crowd roars with laughter as I don't give Tommy a single second's break. I am spurring the little mare and he's hollerin' louder yet. Tommy grabs me tighter around the waist, making the pull on my injured arm harder. Damn, I wish he'd fall off. My arm is killing me, and I'd like to kill the arrogant little son of a gun.

We cross the finish line and the flagger is laughing so hard he can barely sit his horse. Tommy jumps off, yelling what the H is wrong with me. I have tears in my eyes by now, and just turn and ride away. I make it to the trailer, painfully slide off and just sit on the trailer fender and cry. I don't hear him come up until he starts yelling again. I am holding my arm out straight and the splint has torn through the material of my sleeve. Tommy sees it and clamps his mouth shut for a full minute.

"Why didn't you tell me they splinted your arm? What the hell are you doing riding? Folks will think I'm some no-account gunsal when they find out your arm is hurt."

I stare at him. "I'm rodeoing. What are you doing?" I retort.

My folks didn't find out about the arm for a few days. I told them Tommy hurt it when he was trying so hard to climb on my horse. I finally had to go to the doctor when the swelling couldn't be hidden any longer and they realized I couldn't bend it. Turns out my elbow was broken, with a chip broken off of the bone. If I was gonna be hurt I wish it had been due to a bronc instead of a stupid little bull.

Suzy

Suzy is with the football player, the big one with a square jaw and a lot of empty space under his golden curls. He has come over to Chew Corner to see what the "little goat ropers" are doing. It is Spirit Week for Homecoming. Every group or club does something. The Future Farmers of America and the rodeo kids made a bucking barrel. They set four big stout posts deep in the ground and attached the barrel to the posts with cables. This sucker will flat get with it. Bobby put a bare back rigging on it, though I see there's a choice between it and a bull rope. This isn't gonna last long, I'm thinking. The barrel can actually come all the way down to the ground. It can take whoever is on to the ground with it. Not good. Some of the teachers, other than the ag teachers, will have a fit. Suzy is watching Tommy ride, and a couple of other guys who actually do ride rough stock. Riding this barrel ain't easy, I can tell you after watching them.

Suzy's lover-boy decides he is gonna give it a try. This oughta be good. The big goon doesn't have a clue. I don't think he's ever sat on a horse, much less something like this. I see some of the guys exchanging looks, and Suzy catches them. She quietly admonishes them to be nice, rolling her eyes at them and then makes her sweeter-than-honey look.

He jumps on and one of the guys has to exchange

the rigging for the bull rope with him sitting on it. The guy finally tells him to scoot back. He doesn't want to be messing around there. Everyone laughs or snickers. Suzy looks put out and I can tell she is thinking everybody is rude and mean. Like she hasn't pulled stuff and acted that way before.

They have rosined the tar out of the glove and the rope, explaining to him that's what will make him be able to stick and ride. I watch one of them take the rope and make the suicide wrap around the guy's huge hand. He nods and clenches that big ol' square jaw. The barrel goes way high and the jock starts to slide forward, they yell at him to hang on while they whip the barrel around. The barrel is really high in the air now and the football player has slid way off to the side, along with the bull rope. The barrel comes crashing down, on the jock's leg and foot, hitting so hard I wince. Crap.

He hollers in pain and the guys have to help him, he's so heavy he's pinning his own leg down under the barrel. They get him to scoot off the side of the barrel. His foot is an odd angle, and I am thinking it is a good time to be away from this. Especially when I hear someone has gone after the nurse. Suzy is looking at her boyfriend who is now bawling like a calf who can't get to his mama. She walks up to Tommy and punches him in his nose. Then she looks at the crybaby boyfriend and walks away. I see Mr. Nolan, the history teacher and football coach, coming this way at a very fast walk.

He sees me and angles toward me. I am one of his pets. I was the only one who knew the Civil War was really the War Between the States, and that it wasn't based on slavery. I had that stuff drilled into me from the time I could talk, along with "Remember the Alamo", etc. Mr. Nolan is from Georgia originally. He also loves to hunt and is always trying to get an invite to come to our ranch.

Mr. Nolan eyes his star player, and then studies the nurse, assisted by the principal. He asks questions I can't answer. Because I just got there and didn't see anything, I tell him. Having any of his main players injured right before Homecoming is not gonna make him happy. Man, I hope I am convincing. He looks for someone else to ask, and I sneak away.

Chapter Twelve

Gail and Suzy

The heat beats down, it is Nor-Cal in the Sacramento Valley in the summer. The bleachers with a shade over them are packed to capacity. Junior and high school age rodeos always get good attendance. We're sitting beside the arena, our horses are half asleep in the heat. Gail smiles and laughs. I keep quiet. Her boyfriend is out of town, helping the stock contractor put on a different rodeo that he'll also ride in as a contestant. She's telling about the guy she met last week, and how it is so nice to have someone who isn't gone every weekend, and what nice horses he has. I hook my leg around the horn, and I am relieved when Suzy rides up.

Suzy has her trick-riding outfit and saddle on, and will carry the flag while doing a hippodrome stand for the grand entry. I smile at Suzy, hoping Gail has sense enough to shut up while Suzy is here. Gail's boyfriend and Suzy both work for the stock contractor, and Suzy would lose no time carrying tales about Gail. Suzy loves to stir trouble. After trick riding and acting tough, it is her favorite hobby.

Tommy walks up, motioning for the pivot riders to get ready. He also works for the rodeo company, and has lots of responsibilities. He is serious in his duty to keep the show moving, and not get a butt chewing in front of everyone. Tommy reminds me of Popeye. Big arms, and but tiny, like most rough stock riders. His reddish-brown hair and freckles make him look even younger. I heard he is some kind of shirt-tail relative to Lori.

Suzy motions him over, leans over and whispers to him, and I see his eyes settle on Gail. Dang it. Well, Gail should know better. That's no way to behave, anyway. If Suzy calls Gail out about cheating and Gail gets mouthy Suzy'll kick Gail's butt. Suzy is short, and very stout, due to her trick riding. It takes lots of muscle to pull yourself up and around by one arm or leg on a running horse.

Peggy reaches down to make sure her flag boot is secure, squares her shoulders and puts on her big smile. The first notes for the grand entry sound and Tommy holds Suzy's horse while she gets into position. Suzy leads the pivot riders into the arena. I hate carrying a flag, I'm always paranoid something will happen, and the flag will get dropped. My folks, and my Granny and Granddaddy would kick my butt if I ever dropped the flag. I don't let anyone know that every time I hear the anthem, or any patriotic song, a big ol' lump forms in my throat and tears fill my eyes. I am also good at most funerals until Taps plays. I guess it is on account of how I was raised.

Donna rides up, and we talk now that the anthem is over and the arena is cleared. Poor Donna, she's gonna run barrels and poles. Maybe I should say poor horse, all that heavy chest weight leaning one way when she's competing. Peggy and Gail join us, and I bring up the fact Suzy likely heard Gail bragging on the new guy. We warn her she's headed for trouble. The word "alley-cat" comes up. Gail shrugs and pats her horse's butt behind the saddle. "Sometimes, it is nice to have a new ride," she says with a nasty grin. I'd like to wipe that grin off her face.

Donna, Gail, and Me

Donna, Gail and I pull up to the drive-in frosty. Donna needs her coke with extra ice, Gail wants fries and I think I am in need of a vanilla coke. It is weird to see that diamond ring on her finger as she cranks the steering wheel around. Donna has a pickup now that she's married, and obviously pregnant. Her husband drives truck and is rarely around. She gets his pickup and a gas and food allowance while he is working out of town. She is a senior this year, and I wonder if she'll stay in school. Some of the parents are pushing to make her go to the continuation school next to the real high school. They don't want pregnant girls around us—like pregnancy is contagious or something. You can even take your baby to school with you at the continuation school; and join all the pot heads. Donna doesn't belong with that bunch and their "groovy" lifestyle. Donna was not college material, as my Dad used to say. I still hate to see her tied down and married at our age.

The carhop takes our order, her eyes never leaving Donna's lap. Donna has found a halter top that is actually like a peasant style halter top. Since her chest is so large, it is hard for the car hop to see exactly what is below that mountainous ridge. She has heard the rumors, and is trying to see how far along Donna really is. When the carhop returns with the tray of drinks she stalls making change from the coin belt around her thin waist. Donna finally tells her she was gonna say for her to keep it, but she is sure the carhop wants that tip to go to Donna's baby. The girl's eyes widen and she runs back into the building. She wants to be the first to confirm Donna's pregnancy to the other girls.

Donna says her Dad and stepmom are so happy she is out of the house. They can party every night, now. She snorts and says they've had to learn to wash their own dishes and clothes, and mop floors. They were strict jerks to Donna. Despite her stepmom running around with everyone, including sleeping with guys a year or two older than Donna. I always feel like Donna's stepmom is jealous of Donna and wants to prove she is just as desirable as her big-busted stepdaughter. I think of her as being a great example of that old saying about pretty is as pretty does, and the other one about beauty coming from the inside. This woman must be full of rotten crap. Her ugliness could wipe out even Farrah Fawcett's looks.

We are just killing time, doing anything to not be at home. We debate whether we need to go home and get swimming suits and hit the lake or the creek. I look at three sets of bronzed legs, and at the halter tops we have on. Why do we need to go home? Wet undies have never killed us. I mention we can just go to the creek and splash around in what we have on, even go skinny-dipping if we want.

Cold drinks in hand or gripped between our knees,

we burn rubber around the corner and head out of town for the closest creek. Gail shifts for Donna half the time, I hug the door on the curves. I really like Gail, just not half the stuff she does. We drive past the lane that leads to her house. She glances over and begins imitating her sawmill working dad.

"Ya'll better be not up to no good. Girls drivin' 'round in a hot-rod just askin' fer trouble." We giggle. Her folks are like night and day. Gail's mom thinks Gail can do no wrong, and Gail gets every single thing she asks for. Must be nice.

We cross the Sacramento River on the rickety bridge high above the water. The river is huge here, and looks so refreshing. We know better. It is full of undertows and all sorts of hidden dangers. We drive another couple of miles and go to one of the creeks feeding it. We turn left, past the place that will take you fishing with a guide and boat. They sell beer to about anyone and have a couple of good pool tables. Then past the place that cooks the catfish you catch in the river, or you can choose one out of a tank that was caught that day. You can have it fried two different ways, traditional with cornmeal or beer battered. Granddaddy tried them and said they were higher than a cat's back, especially for those who caught their own fish.

We drive another couple of miles, turn off the asphalt onto a dirt road and pull up near the creek. Wild blackberry vines grow along the bank. Pines and oak trees open enough to make a few feet of a beach, and the water is much slower here, almost forming a pool. The water is notoriously cold in this creek. It comes roaring down from the mountains, fed by other mountain streams on its way to the valley. We kick our sandals off and the sand burns our feet. Gail screams and jumps waist deep into the water. I grimace and join her, while Donna slowly inches her way in. "Cowgirl up! Just go under and get it over with!" I yell.

We all dive under and come up in the middle of the creek. "Dang, that's cold!" Gail yells. Donna and I begin to float and we hear a truck pull in further down the creek. Great, we don't need any company, I think. Our shirts and shorts are stuck to us like a second skin. I hope it isn't one of the guys from school. I can only float on my belly, Donna can float in any position. I am thinking there is a couple good reasons for that. Gail is swimming under water. I am looking at the old rope we swing on that hangs over the water when suddenly a dog begins barking frantically downstream. I find my footing and stand up in water that's chest high. I start studying the tangled brushy sides of the creek.

"Oh, crap! Gail, Donna, watch out!" I holler. The dog from the folks downstream has frightened a rattlesnake out of the bushes and the snake is rapidly slithering across the tops of the blackberries. I stare open-mouthed as the snake hits the water. I've never seen one in the water before. The snake looks like a cobra, the first half of his body raised straight out of the water. He looks for something to climb on to get out of the water, and heads towards us! Realizing his intentions, I begin splashing and running for the beach while telling the other girls to run. I see a limb floating out from the banks and throw it behind me, hoping the snake turns and heads for it.

We reach the beach breathless and shaken. The snake must have made it across. I look around us studying the ground just in case. I look at Donna, bent over, with her hands on her knees. I ask if she is okay, and she nods. Gail looks at me, and begins sobbing. Her face screws up and tears begin to fall.

"I will never, ever say anything about you being a hillbilly! I wouldn't have known what to do, that snake would have climbed on me and I'd have just died right there! I mean right there, man! Ginny, you saved our lives! And Donna and her baby, too!" Gail manages to choke the words out between sobs.

I shrug and shake my head. I'm just glad everyone is okay. These valley-raised girls don't see many rattlesnakes; or mountain lions, or bobcats, the stuff I grew up around. I've always caught crap about being a hillbilly since I grew up in the foothills, not down in the valley like them. I went to a two-room school up there, most of my friends attended small town schools in the valley.

PART THREE

Chapter Thirteen

Gail and Me

The church is packed. I don't remember ever seeing that many cars there. Folks have to park way off and walk down the road quite aways. Donna, Lori, Peggy are all sitting together. Their faces look puffy from crying and wads of Kleenex fill their hands. Donna's baby belly fills her lap. There's an empty seat beside them and I try to drop into it without showing the world what my upper thighs look like. I've always hated dresses. I remind myself to keep my legs together. The platform sandals I wear just make the whole thing worse. I hope this preacher isn't real long winded, funerals suck anyway. I am feeling pretty bad about myself.

The preacher drones on, about how important salvation is, and that he is right alongside Gail's family rejoicing that Gail knew the Lord. That he was the one that baptized her in the creek running by this very church not that many years ago. I shut him out, going on about how many lives he has saved as he starts the invitation to come forward and be saved. You'd think the service was about him saving folks, to listen to him. I understand my daddy a bit more, I realize. Daddy doesn't think much of churches. Wow, what a time for me to find out I think like my daddy. Like this whole thing isn't sobering enough.

I think back to the last words I said to Gail, when I told her she was a whore, acting like a damn alley cat. She got caught by her boyfriend, a good local kid, in the camper of one of the bull riders who came for the Pro Rodeo. It tore the kid up, he was so hurt and mad. Heck, he was even crying. Gail laughed at him, in front of the pro bull rider. The bull rider made fun of both Gail and him, saying some pretty awful things. The bull rider had already pulled out of the rodeo grounds when the kid came back with his older brothers, all armed to the teeth. A few weeks later I heard a rumor she was pregnant, and the bull rider wouldn't answer her calls.

Donna told me when she didn't show up to meet her boyfriend he went back to his house and found her laying in his front yard. She said when Gail was found her face was bruised and the hospital didn't know what had happened. The police are investigating it. She also said she heard Gail had a ruptured tubal pregnancy. Along with another rumor the bull rider came back and beat her up.

We didn't know why it happened yet it had. We aren't ready for this kind of thing, friends aren't supposed to die, much less have the question raised if they were killed. Here we are, just dumb kids with some of us making a new life and others leaving this life. This crap isn't supposed to happen to high school kids. The chance to tell Gail I am sorry is gone forever. I silently pray again for both her and God to forgive me.

The singing starts again, the old hymns we were raised on. The Old Rugged Cross, In the Garden, I'll Fly Away; songs about redemption and salvation. The preacher raises his arms and asks for everyone to rise and file around the casket to say our final goodbyes, while reminding us it is only a shell of her left, that Gail has indeed flown away to a better place.

I follow my friends and get in line as we are told to do. I peer around the row of people and realize the casket is open. No, please God, no. I don't want to see her like this. I step back in line and keep my head bowed, staring at the floor. I realize the boys who are pallbearers are white and pasty. They've had to sit and stare at Gail the whole time. I feel bad for Tommy and Bobby, along with the others. I know none of them had to take turns sitting with her the last couple of days, at least. Gail's family members did that. Sometimes the constable or a county deputy would sit with the men sitting with the dead, too. Shuffling along in line I feel like a hypocrite. I would give anything to take back the words I said to Gail. When I get to the casket I manage to glance at Gail, and see the bruise on one side of her face, running into her neck. I don't want to look again, but I am wondering why makeup wasn't applied to cover it. I also think that bruise shouldn't have been there. Doesn't embalming remove all the blood? I know from science classes that bruises or hematomas are nothing but pools of blood. Gail is dressed in her last prom dress, and even has a corsage pinned on it. Dang, she'll never dance again, I think, my lip quivering. My legs shake. I want to throw up.

Donna

I am on the front porch when I see Donna coming down the road. She parks in front of my house, and then reaches around and grabs the baby. She still looks bad. I know it isn't easy for her. It hasn't been easy for any of us. She and Gail were best friends since they were toddlers. Their folks and grandparents came out here from Oklahoma together.

Donna shifts the baby to her other bony hip. The Ditto brand pants she has on are probably a dang size zero. She's never had any hips, butt, or thighs and is really thin from the waist down now. Shoot, her flanks are empty, like a cow that hasn't watered. She smiles, follows me into the house, and props the baby on the couch.

I'm glad my folks are gone to look at some investment property.

I attempt to smile at the baby. I'm uncomfortable with babies. I've never been around them much, and do not baby sit. Ever.

Donna says she just left her folks place, well, her dad and stepmom's place. She looks up at me and then says she forgets, tears filling her eyes. Just plain forgets that Gail is gone. Says she told her folks bye when she was getting ready to leave, and said she was going to Gail's. She had just stopped by so they could see the baby on the way.

I wait, my chest hurting. Donna's witch of a stepmom yelled at her that Gail was gone, stone dead. Told Donna she is crazy, she'd better get over Gail being gone. She'll end up like Gail's mom, a real fruitcake.

Gail's mom hasn't left the house since Gail's funeral.

Donna's lip trembles while she tells me she knows Gail is gone. Donna even took her turn sitting with Gail in her casket. Oh, man, I didn't know Donna did that. I thought it was always men who sat with the dead. Donna explains through tears that it is just a habit that she'd say she was going to see Gail.

I think back to when I heard Gail was in the hospital. They said her boyfriend found her in the yard, passed out. The hospital was asking for blood, she was bleeding internally, her spleen was ruptured, and she was still in a coma. I told my folks I was going to go donate blood the next day, then got word they had enough blood. I decided I'd better go see her, at least. I knew she was in a coma. Someone told me folks in comas could still hear, they just couldn't respond to anything. The next morning it was too late, she was gone. I remember going out to the barn and staring up at the old rafters through streaming tears and asking her to forgive me for all I'd done and said. I felt responsible, like I had a hand somehow in her dying.

I realize Donna is talking, and force myself back to

reality. I manage to tell her she isn't nuts. She tells me she's tried talking to Gail's folks. Gail's dad finally told her to not call or come by. It upsets Gail's mom too much, it reminds her Gail is gone and Donna is still here. I figure Donna feels like there is anyone to share her grief.

I don't know why I am beginning to see and think these things. Like me understanding my daddy and Donna. I am afraid it is part of growing up. I'm not sure I want to grow all the way up.

Donna looks at me and tells me that Gail had forgiven me, that I should know that. That Gail was going to come make up with me the day they found her.

I shut my eyes, and clench my hands before wrapping my arms around myself. I hope God can forgive me, too. I feel Donna wrap her arms around me and we cry until both of us have wet shoulders.

Once again, she tells me about Gail's face being bruised and the hospital not knowing what had happened, how the police investigated. About the rumor the bull rider beat her up. I steel myself and let her talk. I figure she might be thinking if she repeats it often enough she'll begin to believe Gail is really gone.

We all hate that it happened. When my granddaddy heard about Gail he solemnly told me the old must die and the young will. Like that great philosophy helps. I guess he has seen his share of dying.

Donna asks if I will go with her to Gail's grave. It

is up in the hills under a big old oak tree. I don't want to go, but something inside me tells me I need to go, for Donna, if nothing else.

More of that dang growing up stuff, I realize.

Chapter Fourteen

Me

Peggy's mom, Sandy, gets in line behind me at the grocery store. I try to smile as Sandy says hello. I ask how Peggy is doing in school, and fib and say I haven't talked to her for a while. Peg won a great scholarship and is rodeoing in both the state and college associations. She's also dating one of her professors, and I am willing to bet Sandy doesn't know about the professor.

Sandy starts in on how Peggy could be number one in the state for barrels if she'd just try harder, and how it is the same with her classes. Heaven's sake, she's only holding a 3.8 in school and that has to change, she tells me with pursed lips. I watch her red chalky lipstick end up in lines like whiskers and find myself wishing she had a tail I could step on. She's too much like the cat that happily purrs on your lap before digging in with her claws.

My items are rung up and the clerk leans in and whispers "Bless her heart, poor Peggy." I nod and help the box boy loading my groceries into the cart. That's the trouble with small towns. Everybody knows everything.

Feeling the need for fresh air I go outside quick as I can and jump off the high old sidewalk. I turn to get my groceries from the high sidewalk ledge. A pair of snake-skin boots appear next to the brown paper bags. My eyes travel up past the starched khakis to the plaid shirt shot with gold threads. It is one of my dad's old business partners. He runs a big real estate office and has the usual toothpick in his mouth and his expensive hat pushed back off his face.

"What's that ol' daddy of yours up to?" he asks as he clinches a toothpick. His teeth are yellowed from drinking West Texas water in his youth.

I look away before replying. He doesn't know Dad's fallen off the wagon. Thirteen years of sobriety all gone. Dad had a pretty bad stroke and when he was told he had bleeding in his brain that there was no way of stopping, he said to hell with it. He'd live his life as he saw fit. Which included being a raging drunk a good amount of the time. Mama made him sell the cows and ranch I was born on and buy investment property "to relive stress". Yeah, right. Everyone knew she'd jump at the chance to get back into town and her bridge games. Funny that the stroke didn't happen 'til after he sold the ranch and cows.

"He's staying busy," I smile and hope that will suffice.

It doesn't.

"How come you're back home? To help your folks? I heard he had a stroke. Nothing will keep that man down for long, everyone knows that. I hope you took my advice to heart about thinking long and hard 'fore settling down. Remember, it is just as easy to love somebody with money as a poor boy. Hell, you don't even have to love 'em—just like 'em a lil' bit!" He thinks he is real funny and guffaws at his own joke.

"Yes, sir, I remembered what you said. I just came home for a bit, needed a break and needed to help my folks out."

He nods again and finally starts walking away. Man, I have to get out of here, somehow. Away from this small town.

Donna and Me

It has been a few months since graduation. I have hardly seen or heard from anyone much until Donna called for me to meet her at the frosty this evening. She's moved out of town and I haven't heard from her in a while. We find a place to park in the shade to drink our cokes and ended up sitting on one of the picnic tables under a scraggly eucalyptus tree, hoping to catch a breeze. Seven o'clock and still above 100 degrees. We were both sticky with sweat and tired.

Donna asks if I know Lori left town. I ask where she's going to school, assuming that's why she's gone. Donna says she doesn't think it is college related, and is wondering if it has something to do with Gail. Maybe something we don't know about? I can't look at Donna, and feel a tear slide down my face. I wonder if Donna will ever get over Gail dying.

"They weren't that close, I wouldn't think so," I finally manage to say without looking at Donna. Donna doesn't respond and we both sip our cokes in silence. "She's probably wanting to get to a new place, a bigger town or something. She always said she couldn't wait to get out of Hickville. Especially after the wreck and her former friends, the stupid cheerleaders and jocks were so hateful to her," I add.

"You do know about Suzy's boyfriend, don't you?" she asks me pointedly. I know she's trying to emphasize the fact I don't keep up with everybody, and that I've turned into a loner. Hell, I can hardly manage my own life. I don't need to know what everybody else is doing.

"What now?" I ask, exasperated.

"You know that bunch she runs with is getting into drugs? Her boyfriend Steve, I think you met him a couple of times. The one who thought he was God's gift to women? Yeah, well, his folks got him out of rehab and brought him back to the ranch there in the mountains. They went to some dang cow camp the next day and left him home. Steve's buddy, Buster, came out a couple of days later. Buster saw things weren't right soon as he pulled into headquarters. Chores and stuff hadn't been done. Buster went on into the house and found him in his bedroom. The autopsy showed he overdosed on that Angel Dust."

"Really. Oh, man. Well, I hope this wakes Suzy up. Talk about a Come to Jesus. I hate for that to happen to anyone. Good Lord, what kind of people are his folks? Leaving someone just out of rehab all alone like that. I didn't like him and knew he was bad news. But, poor Suzy," I shake my head in disbelief.

Donna nods and says "Yep. One more thing. Peggy is trying to get ahold of you. She's getting married and we're in the wedding."

Guess life is going on and everyone is moving forward. No matter what. More for some than others. I still can't figure out how I am going to afford to go to college, even with the scholarship. My folks refuse to give me any help. They say if I want it bad enough, I will find a way.

Donna is back in town, I hear. Maybe visiting, no one is sure. She has all three kids with her, and no husband. They moved away a couple of years ago, started their own trucking business. Donna used to call, saying how lonely she was with him on the road all the time. They made good money. She had everything she wanted except a husband and a father to help with the kids.

Donna calls my folks and gets my number. She wants me to come to her folks' place. I dread seeing her folks, but I do finally agree. When I walk into the farmhouse that smells of cheap cigarettes and old grease, I see her Dad sitting at the table, smoking. His straw hat is pushed back and I see the red spider webs on his face from too much drinking. He has a half-eaten tomato sandwich on a chipped plate, along with a big ol' slice of red onion. Donna's youngest kid has a squashed mess of white bread, tomato and mayo on her plate. And in her sparse white hair. He tells Donna she needs to clean her up, like no one is aware of this. Donna grabs her and takes her to the old enamel kitchen sink and drainboard. I stand there, not sure what to do, and finally grab the dishrag and start to wipe the table. There's a bowl of cucumbers sitting in ice and vinegar that has spilled on the oilcloth. He asks if I want any of it, he'll have Donna make me a sandwich. I thank him, politely decline, and pick up on the fact his wicked wife must not be home.

Donna asks if I want to go get a coke. We escape to her fancy new car. After trying to help her get three kids in the back seat, we lose no time bumping down the popular lined drive. Donna doesn't turn her head to tell me she is looking for a place to rent. She is done with her husband. He decided the best way to not miss his family was to make other families, all over the country. I don't know what to say. I look out the windshield at the pastures and fence posts rolling by. Damn. I'd always heard truckers were known to have women in every town, and sometimes whole families. Donna turns onto the road that leads to town and heads for the frosty. Says she is thirsty and she wants to see if anyone is there from our old bunch.

A new carhop appears at the window and I order my usual vanilla coke, and Donna her coke with extra ice. Donna looks around and asks if any of the old gang ever come here. I tell her I don't know, I am rarely in town anymore. After the carhop leaves the tray on Donna's window, Donna passes me the drink with the V on the lid. She then grabs hers, takes a big drink, then places it between her knees and reaches in the jockey box. She pulls out a bottle of vodka and fills her cup, drinking some and pouring more in before she replaces the lid and straw. I watch and realize my mouth has fallen open when she giggles and asks if I catch many flies doing that.

"Let's go to the yard," she says as she waves the gal over to take the tray away. Suzy works there and I am wondering who Donna is wanting to see. Suzy works in both the western store and the actual cattle pens. It is the largest livestock auction yard west of the Rockies, or the Mississippi. One of the two, I can't remember which. Back when we were in high school we'd cut classes and go to the yard, dodging our daddies who were usually there. The cafe stays open 24 hours due to the huge sales and cattle trucks coming and going at all hours. We'd go to the cafe after the dances for breakfast, too. They made good pies, piled high with calf slobbers or oozing fruit out of the flaky crust.

Suzy is riding a little dappled gray horse when we pull up by the tag shed. She's got on pretty fancy clothes for riding pens. She also models for the western store here. I happened to be there one time when a cattle buyer asked her to try something on, since it appeared she was the same size as his wife. I saw him slip her his hotel key when he handed his money over to buy the outfit he had her try on for him.

She rides other folk's horses, so she gets double

paid, by the horse owner for training and by the yard for working the cattle. No one ever rides their own horse there on the cement pens if they think anything of the horse. While it is a good place for a horse to learn, I sure wouldn't want my horse there for very long. It has been rumored Suzy is still drinking too much and using drugs, like her rough stock buddies she always hangs with. Suzy squints at Donna's truck and watches as we get out. "Well, look at what the cat drug in!" she says with a big smile. She gets off the horse and loops the reins around a post before she comes over to see us.

"What are ya'll doing? I heard you was back in town, Donna," she says with a questioning look.

Donna tells her she's looking for a place to rent and she's left her ol' man. She asks Suzy to call her folks number if she hears of anything. She'd like a place with pasture for the show horses she's hung onto. Suzy looks over at the car and the kids' heads bobbing around in the back seat. She's probably wondering what a twenty-two-year-old with three kids is gonna do. The same thing I wonder.

Chapter Fifteen

Me

I've swept the barn, and get out the supplies I need to wash the sorrel mare. I've got everything except the Beer On Tap shampoo. The mare is new and rolls her eyes at the hose I've stretched out. At least she hasn't stamped her feet at it. I can always tell a horse who has been around rattlesnakes. They stamp their feet at hoses. The folks I work for probably wouldn't like my choice of shampoo, yet nothing will shine a horse up like this brand. The reason this horse looks like a shiny copper penny is the shampoo I use. I scratch the mare's neck and keep talking to her while I slowly turn on the water. The plastic brush is attached to the hose and I begin letting the water run on her legs. She begins to relax and doesn't give me any trouble. By the time I've worked my way over her shoulders. I'm talking to her and moving slow but relaxed like Granddaddy taught me. I don't hear the owner come in, instead I feel the horse tense and see her ears prick. I figure someone or something has come in.

The owner grins at me as I slowly follow the mare's stare. I remember I have that bottle of shampoo inside the bucket and hope he doesn't see it. This is a fancy place, they think they have to buy the most expensive stuff, and sometimes that high dollar stuff doesn't work that well. He stays in the doorway, arms folded across his starched white shirt.

"I've been watching you. You're doing exactly what I want, taking your time and allowing her to get used to things. Keep it up." He tips his hat at me and turns on his heel to leave.

I feel sweat running down my neck. I can't afford to lose this job. It would mean I'd probably have to move home, where I am not wanted and where I don't want to be, either. The couple that have this place just moved here from Colorado, though the wife is from Texas. She is always all dolled up, big hair, fancy clothes and lots of jewelry. I can smell her perfume before I ever see her. The man is nice, I am not sure the wife likes me around. She is pretty sure everyone is after her husband. I make dang sure I am nothing but business-like with him.

Donna and Me

Donna has talked me into going to the bar. She got a neighbor kid to watch her kids so she can have a night out. I really don't care much about going, I am tired. I spent a good part of the day tying colts to the fence and leading them to water, part of their training for being halter broke and learning to stand. Some were pretty ignorant and not fast learners, and the snotty fancy-pants wife came down several times to watch me. She just stood there watching without a single change in her painted-up face until she got bored, I guess. It just makes me tense to have her around and I know that tenseness transfers to the horses. It wears me out, too.

Donna and I find a couple of empty stools and I turn it so I can slide onto the seat. I swear every man in the place is watching as Donna tries to fit into the space and get up on the stool. Even I'm mashed by her chest as she tries to get onto the stool. We order drinks and they're already paid for. Of course, they are, when Donna's with you. I should have ordered the best whiskey, dang it.

I sip at the whiskey sour and stare into the mirror behind the bar. I watch as some couples get up to dance to the jukebox. I hear a giggle I haven't heard in a while and turn around. Yep, it is Lori. Her partner swings her around. I watch as her perfect hair gets mashed. It sticks to her partner's sleeve when the guy doesn't lift his arm high enough while he whirls her around. She doesn't giggle now. That's like a cardinal sin to her. No one messes with Lori's hair, that's an unspoken law. She does manage a fake smile and I can tell she's telling him to be more careful.

I lean over to Donna and ask if she has spotted Lori. Donna says Lori is here all the time. That the guy is loaded and buys Lori everything she wants. I bite back the response that self-respect and dignity can't be bought. I'm as sour as the drink in my hand. I reckon living here will do that.

A short glass of green stuff is placed in front of me. I silently groan. One of the old coots has sent me a crème de menthe, their idea of a lady's drink. Dang, this ain't Dixie and I am no southern belle. The crap tastes like bad cough syrup. I feel a hand grab my shoulder and look up to see Tommy telling me we need to dance. I turn the stool around and join him on the dance floor, happy it is a fast dance. We dance a bit separately before he grabs me and we begin the twirling dance that is known as the Okie Stomp. When the last notes of Proud Mary fade away, I turn to head back for the bar. He stops me, and I find myself in his arms for Silver Wings. Oh, well, his aftershave is pretty good and I allow my head to rest on his shoulder. I did say I am tired, after all. Tommy is one of the few people I know I can actually lean on.

Chapter Sixteen

Peggy and Me

The ancient oak trees are shiny and green, their branches laden with wisteria draping down. I feel the moisture from the greener-than-green grass begin to soak my nylon-covered toe. You'd think platform sandals would keep you far enough above the ground. I fidget with the bouquet I hold. Peggy did all the flowers for her own wedding. She'd started working at the florist last year, when she came home from college. The flowers are really pretty, but I've admired them long enough. I sure wish they'd get this show on the road, as my granddaddy would say. The peasant style bridesmaid dress I am wearing is beginning to itch from the crocheted lace on my chest, and I think I can feel the flower thing pinned in my fine, short hair begin to slide down.

At last the music starts and Peggy's husband-to-be-real-soon starts coming up to the alter with his groomsmen. I am glad we bridesmaids didn't have to be escorted up there like they do in some weddings. I see a couple of birds land in the tree above me, and hope they don't decide to decorate any of us standing below. I see Sandy, Peggy's mom, pretending she's wiping a tear with a fancy hanky. She makes sure to let a little sob escape loud enough to get attention. Peggy's daddy is waiting to walk her up the aisle.

Sandy pretty much chose her daughter's husband, Jim. He seems nice enough, a little older, a team roper who builds big, fancy houses for all the folks moving up here from L.A. and the Bay area. To God's Country, they say. Problem is, they want to turn it into where they came from and consider us all backwards Okies and hicks. Peggy's granny asked Jim who his people were, like she does everyone she meets. She was able to figure out who they were, and when he called her ma'am and took his hat off, it didn't matter much who his people were, anyway. She knew he was raised right, by folks who came out here from where manners were still taught and practiced.

The ceremony over, I head for the tables set up under the trees, laden with barbecue beef, beans, salads and about every kind of covered dish. At the end is the huge wedding cake that Sandy had to tell everyone how much it cost. I am looking for the tables with the keg. I finally see it and the table with all the bottles of wine. Guess Sandy was out to impress her new son-in-law's clients with the collection of California wine. I am thinking the extent of her knowledge concerning wine is that she probably just knows the wines come in colors.

Holding my dress in one hand and a cup of beer in the other I watch as the toddler ring-bearer trips the little flower-girl and they roll in the wet grass. The boy's white shirt and the little girl's lacey dress already show grass stain streaks. I hear the "bless their hearts, they're just plumb wore out," as someone separates the kids. The little girl has knocked the crap out of the boy. I see blood on his white shirt. Way to learn early, I silently cheer on the little girl. I head for my truck where I will get my jeans and boots. I can't wait to shuck the dress and platform shoes. It's gonna be a big party tonight, and I ain't about to be trying to dance in a long dress and these shoes on this wet grass. Some of the boys throw you into a spin pretty hard. I don't want to end up on my fanny.

Suzy and Me

The crowd is going wild, the gal is spurring the mechanical bull. I make my way to where I can see. I should have known. It is Suzy. She jumps off and takes a bow. She spots me and comes over, grabbing my beer and taking a swig. She's out of breath and reaches down to show me her ankle. She had on platform sandals and has worn the nylon of her panty hose clean through on her ankle, the skin is red and burned-looking. We wear the dang hose to keep from getting panty lines in our new style jeans that don't have back pockets. Dittos, is what they're called. When she looks up at me, I see her eyes. Damn, they look like doll's eyes. She's on something, again. I heard some of the people she's been hanging with are snorting coke. I doubt she will ever learn what not to do.

Before I can say anything, a guy shows up, grabs her around the shoulders and whispers in her ear. She smiles and nods. He saunters off with his cocky hat adorned with an eagle feather. Suzy tells me she's got to go on a diet, it was hard to ride that stupid thing. She is short, solid muscle. She might be a little bigger than what she was a couple of years ago in school, but she's still not fat. Suzy says she's taking some diet pills but it isn't enough. I figure she probably knows I know she's on something. That's why she's saying she's on diet pills.

The band starts up with a song about looking for love in all the wrong places. Yeah, the story of my life, and everyone in here, I think sourly. Finding love in a smoky honky-tonk full of "urban cowboys" ain't exactly the place you'll find anyone worth their salt. Suzy nods good bye and heads outside, I'm betting to meet the guy. I hear "Hey, Ginny!" and feel my belt loop being jerked on. It is Buster, trying to pull me out on the dance floor.

Buster moved up from the Central Valley a couple of years ago. He's related to some of the folks up here. He is the only one besides my family who calls me Ginny. It is spelled with a G, sounds like a J. He wasn't around for the high school nicknames, thank God. He places my beer on a table and we begin dancing a waltz. His aftershave smells good and I relax as we make our way across the floor. When the dance is over he keeps hold of my hand and walks me back to the table. Guess his mama taught him something.

Donna and Me

I hang up the last halter and am about to shut the saddle room door when the phone rings. It is Donna, wanting to meet. I will have to tell her again not to call here. Miss Prissy Pants Owner already made a comment about the barn phone being strictly for business. Mostly for her to call and give me orders and make sure what was going on when her husband is down here at the barn. He's rarely around me, though she thinks different. I don't need or want the headache of a married man, even if he is good looking and nice.

I don't bother to clean up, or shower. I really don't care if I smell like horses. It is who I am. I have gotten into Donna's truck and see the white paper bag already soaking through with grease. It smells great, and I thank her for picking up food. I reach for another fry while Donna rattles the ice in her coke. She's full of information this evening. I had no idea Tommy and Lori had eloped. They ran off to Reno, she said. We were all surprised when Lori came back after being gone almost a year. She'd gone to an aunt's to work in the city, and we all figured that's where she'd stay. Where there were lots of guys to smile at and flirt with, and lots of the excitement that she always seemed to crave. Heck, I didn't even know Tommy was dating her. They weren't a likely match. He was down to earth and always worrying about doing things right, and she was such a prissy, fluffy gal. Besides, last time I saw her she was with Mr. Moneybags at the bar.

Donna studies me and asks me if I am ever gonna get married. I look at her and say just because everyone else was doesn't mean I have to. I also mention I am pretty happy with my dogs and horses, you don't have to worry about them cheating on you or developing a drinking or drug program. Donna of all people ought to know the pitfalls of marriage, I don't need her lecture, either. Everyone else does plenty of that.

"You know those horses and cows you love so much ain't gonna keep you warm at night, or give you kids," she tells me.

I want to ask who is keeping her bed warm since her divorce, but I restrain myself. I won't be catty this time. I am really working on not being that way. Maybe someday I will marry, I finally tell her. As long as I don't have to live at home, I am good. Over twenty years of the Yankee vs. Southerner, city vs. country relationship of my parents was more than enough. Crap, I should be the alcoholic instead of my dad. I go see my grandparents on my dad's side every week, and drop by my folks once in a while. I am not ready for anything more right now. Family goes a lot further than most folks know. And having kids is nowhere on my list.

"You will be wanting someone one day. Being alone ain't good. I just hope it won't be too late," she tells me primly.

I snort and reply. "Twenty-two isn't old! I'm doing what I want right now. Maybe I'll feel different someday. The only person I have to rely on is myself, and that's proven to be pretty good so far."

I hope my show of bravado will quiet her for a while. Just the other day I was at Granny and Granddaddy's, sitting on the porch helping with snapping beans and drinking sweet tea when the subject of me marrying came up. Sure seems to be a popular subject lately. There were times when I felt it would be nice to have someone, I've spent much of my life pretty much alone, not having any brothers or sisters, living way out on the ranches. And I sure don't want a marriage like my folks—nothing in common and fighting half the time. Granny and Granddaddy provided most of the love and affection in my life. When I was a kid the minute I came in their door candy, tea, pop, whatever they had baked or fixed was offered to me with a hug. They gave me real love.

PART FOUR

The School of Harder Knocks

Chapter Seventeen

Me

I pull over to the mailbox sitting on the highway, letting the dust settle on the fifteen miles of dirt road behind me. I only come after the mail a couple of times a week. We're struggling to make ends meet and can't afford the thirty-mile round trip just to get the mail. I stop and open the over-sized mailbox sitting on a cedar post just past the cattle guard. I see a letter from back home and rip it open. I scan it, trying to get to the bottom to see who actually wrote me. It is from Peggy and full of news about the old bunch. Honestly, I haven't thought about them in a while. Life here is so different. It takes everything I have to just get through a day sometimes.

Peggy writes that Suzy is divorced. No surprise there. That Peg sells her artwork, earning quite a name for herself in that circle. Peggy hasn't seen anything of Donna in a long while. Lori and Tommy have built a fancy place, the kind you see in magazines, then she tells me more about, "the perfect couple." Tommy is using the college education he started on, and developed an impressive feed line for livestock. Lori is the social butterfly, entertaining folks at their home.

The next line says that Bobby tried to kill himself by shooting himself and has some brain damage from the gun shot. Evidently, he had been after Lori, was crazy in love with her. He tried to get her to leave Tommy, even while Tommy would be in the next room. Lori finally had to tell Tommy his best friend was trying to get her to leave him. Tommy confronted him and told him their friendship was over and he'd kill him if he ever heard of Bobby coming around or calling there. Bobby got drunk and tried to save Tommy the trouble, shot himself in the temple with a 22. The doctors figured Bobby might relearn some things eventually.

My eyes fill with tears. Good God. I lay the letter on the seat beside me and sit and stare at the blue mountains and high, cold desert surrounding me. A chill runs through me. This high desert is a long way from that warm valley town. There's no fancy flowers here, no tree-lined streets and white painted fences. It is sixty-five miles to buy a loaf of bread. That little town, those people I thought I left behind were brought here with me, are forever a part of me and won't ever leave. Physical distances mean nothing, I realize. The hurry to escape years ago didn't help. I didn't know it would follow me forever.

I jump when I hear a horn. I see a hunter is sitting in his pickup behind me. I have no idea how long he has been sitting there. I pull a hanky out of my pocket and wipe my eyes while I throw the truck into gear and pull over. I don't look at the hunter, just turn my head away and crank the truck around to head home. I don't need him asking me where the big deer are.

I remember my knees were shaking as I stood at the altar. I really didn't want to be standing there, getting married to Buster. It was a way to get out of here, to have a life away from what we discovered was known as Okieville. Once we got out in the world, went to college, or got jobs and began to spread our fragile wings, we found out. The hard way, most often. Some folks laughed at our manners, at our yes sirs and yes ma'ams, said we had accents. It stung. We were considered hicks. Sometimes, I wish I hadn't stood at that altar, wished I hadn't pledged to God and everyone else to keep those dang vows. But, I did, and I'd have to honor them. It just seems there is a whole lot worse than better in my marriage.

I am sitting at the table with my kids, trying to keep them busy with coloring. Every time one of the dogs begins to bark, they look up, eagerly anticipating their daddy coming home. I hate this crap. I hope they are in bed before he arrives. If he even comes home tonight. I dread the smell of the booze, the staggering and not knowing what mood he will be in. Slobbering with lust or raging with anger. After every stall tactic known to children, the kids are finally in bed. Once again, I lie to them, tell them he probably had a flat tire, he found a sick cow, the fence was down, any of the stories I've learned to fabricate so they don't go to bed worrying about him. I wonder why I still worry. Maybe for them, I don't know. The drunk I am married to has little in common to the kid I married, the fresh-faced kid with so many goals and dreams. I like to believe he still is in there, and will reappear someday. That he can manage to fight his way out of the piss poor man that has that good boy hidden deep within him. I read an article in one of the cattle magazines last week that said alcoholism was highest in the agriculture field. The more remote the farm or ranch, the higher incidence there is in alcohol related suicide and fatal accidents. I think back to how I grew up, and how alcohol had always played a role in my life. Granddaddy going off on a drunk every time family came from out of the area or from back in Texas. I had heard stories of how one of my great grandfathers always got crap-faced after making the long drive down the trail to Ft. Worth to load his cattle. That was the only time he ever drank, once a year when he rode the train with his cattle to the stockyards.

There were Daddy's escapades. The time he and I were coming back to Mama's house in town and we'd stopped at a bar where I got a Shirley Temple for every beer he drank. We woke up in a field the next morning. I had a goose egg on my forehead from hitting the dash and Daddy was sore and stiff. We'd gone down a hill and through two fences before the truck came to rest. I was four years old. Daddy got the truck started and we went on to see Mama, driving the rest of the way staring through a badly shattered windshield. She never even looked for us or called anyone to go look. When Granny and Granddaddy found out, they were furious, at both Daddy and Mama. Mama just shrugged when Granny hissed at her, demanding to know how she could not worry about her little daughter missing all night. It seemed Mom quit caring a long time ago.

Donna and Me

Buster and I are sitting on the porch, drinking tea after a long day of haying. It has been a few years since he's had anything stronger than his God-awful coffee, and I am grateful for that. He's finally been able to stay on the wagon. We see a long line of dust; the sign a car is coming to the remote part of the world we call home. We wonder who it will be, we weren't expecting anybody. The kids are all in town, for school and with jobs. A white pickup rolls up in a cloud of dust. It stops under the old Chinese elm trees. I make out the California plates and a heavy chested blonde woman climbs out and comes around the truck. "Geez, it's Donna!" Buster exclaims.

She is thin, her chest by far the largest part of her. Her skin shows ravages of the 1970s, laying under the sprinklers coated with baby oil until a deep golden brown developed like our Grannys' roasted hens. She pushes sunglasses up on her bleached white hair and gives us her trademark grin as we meet her at the yard gate.

"Bet you all weren't expecting me!" she says as she reaches out to hug us. I figure back to how many years since we saw her, how many kids ago, how many life changes. She plops down beside us and I see her cold drink cup. I offer her some tea, apologize for our appearance and our probable odor of sweat and diesel mixed with grass. She says she's fine, filled her cup before she got here and we know dang well that being dirty from working is nothing to be ashamed of. We find out she is on her way back from CA, she has lived in Oklahoma the last decade. Her daddy passed away and she went back to help bury him. We are stunned, and tell her we hadn't heard about her dad. Donna explains that her step mama didn't tell her he was sick until it was too late. Donna also went to see her kids; she'd ended up leaving them years ago for their daddy to raise. She said she'd go back to see them on most holidays. They don't really care much about seeing her. Their lives are busy and it is hard for them to make time to visit when she goes back to California. She lost her last husband, he did leave her his oil and gas rights, so she is all right financially.

Buster and I exchange looks. It is a lot to digest. I get up to get more tea and when I return Donna has a bottle of vodka sitting on the porch railing. Crap, not what I need. I don't want Buster drinking again. I try to steal a look at Buster's glass. It looks the same and I breathe a bit easier. Donna, booze, and old times could be a real lethal mix.

Suzy

Suzy steps into the motor home and locks the door behind her. She goes to the closet and finds the red white and blue fringed costume she'll wear for this evening's performance. The white tennis shoes are below it and as she reaches for them, and sees the bottle behind a pair of boots. She stops, looks away and slides the door closed. Stepping into the bathroom she wiggles her jeans down and frowns at the small belly released from the tight jeans. She sighs. It seems pointless to try to keep the belly in control. She isn't a teenager anymore. She's been trick riding since she was five years old, hell, she's been doing it so long people are shocked she still does it. The medicine cabinet beckons silently. She shakes out a couple of pills. She can chase the pills with the booze, that will work, she decides.

Ron waits at the gate as Suzy completes her final lap around the arena. She climbs back into the saddle, slips her feet into the foot holds and stands, waving at the crowd as she speeds toward the gate. Ron catches her horse by the sequined bridle. Suzy looks down and nods, sliding back into the saddle seat, her feet finding the stirrups. He glances up at Suzy's face, noting the dust sticking to the shiny sweat, the blue eyes too large and unblinking, the smile practiced and meaningless. The crowd is still applauding as he leads the dancing horse out the gate. She slips off the horse once they are clear of the others. She feels her knees weaken and grabs for the saddle to steady herself. Ron doesn't turn around, just keeps leading the horse back to the motor home and trailer. Suzy leans on the horse, trying to be nonchalant as she walks beside the horse, smiling and nodding as they meet other riders.

Ron slips the bridle off and buckles the halter in its place. With his back still to Suzy he tells her she can stop faking it. He ties the horse before he slowly turns around.

"How stupid do you think I am? And how long do you think it will be before you screw up bad? I saw you get out of time tonight. Don't you think the contractor did, too? Stop playing games, damn it. I know about the bottles, you're on something else tonight. I can't stand by and watch you get hurt, or hurt this poor damn horse. Your own brother is worried about you. Luke and I had a talk the other day. You are asking too much of the folks who care about you."

"I don't know what you're talking about, Ronnie. I did fine tonight. Did you hear the crowd? They loved it. You're imagining things, honey." She gave him her best smile, letting her face crinkle at her eyes. She fought to keep the panic from showing. She couldn't feel her legs, she was still holding onto the saddle but trying to appear as if she were just relaxing, leaning on the horse. She felt her heart thumping, wondering if he could see. It was thumping so hard it felt like it was coming out of her chest. She looked down to see if it really was. The ground was swimming, and then she saw her heart come tearing out of her chest, big and red, pumping blood all over her white shoes. Oh, no, she thought, this isn't right. She tried to tell Ronnie, but her mouth wouldn't work. She saw the ground coming up to hit her before she passed out.

Chapter Eighteen

Peggy

Peggy tries to hold back the tears. Her mother's car is still in the driveway, but already backing out. "I'll be damned if I allow that woman to make me cry again!" she said to the empty room. Sandy dropped by her daughter's place and found out Peggy was going to make her a grandmother. Sandy spat out hateful words, words that couldn't be taken back. She was not old enough to be a damn grandmother, how dare Peggy. After all Mike and Sandy had done to help Peggy, and this was the way their sacrifices were shown appreciation? Sandy had then pointed to the not yet finished painting on the easel. It was of a young girl riding a pony alongside a man smiling down fondly from his much taller horse. Sandy went on, saying that was why it wasn't finished, and not good at all, the stupid pregnancy. Those hormones and morning sickness sure weren't going to help Peggy if she ever wanted to become a real painter. That kind of work was a joke, as was the subject. Peggy needed to face the fact that her life was off-track and going nowhere. She needed to leave the playing around with art alone and concentrate on her husband since she was starting to look fat and pasty.

"These unrealistic paintings of yours are so amateur and childish. Just like your oh-so special Daddy's mama. You all are just dreamers, you both dream you have talents neither of you will ever have." Sandy gathered steam and continued on her roll. "The truth is always best, instead of some fantasy land that will eventually break your heart when you find out none of it is real. Your dad never looked at you like that, or even rode with you that often." Sandy had said while pointing a highly polished fingernail at the painting. Peggy muttered she was going to be sick, hoping Sandy would leave. She really did feel sick and wished she could puke all over Sandy's new expensive boots. Sandy made a face at the thought of Peggy getting sick and headed for the door, slamming it on her way out. Peggy instinctively placed her hands on the small mound below her waist. She'd not allow anyone to do to her baby what had been done to her as a child. No one would ever tell her child it wasn't good enough. She soberly realized it hadn't ever stopped, and wouldn't, unless she stopped it herself.

Peggy lifts the shirt to her face staring at it. Her heart pounds as she smells it and stares at the faint pink on the collar. She closes her eyes and tears begin to slide down her face. The perfume, and the lip gloss are proof of what she has denied, what she already knows, but keeps pushing down deep inside. Damn him. All to hell.

She always tries so hard. Keeps the house he built for them spic and span, has a good dinner on the table for him every night. She's planted trees, shrubs, made flowerbeds that are the envy of their neighbors. She makes sure their daughter, Robin, does well in school, had taught her manners and taught her to ride and even rope, since he is gone so much. He is always having to work late to make sure his crew finishes in time or has to meet with clients in the evening. Peggy has put her own riding, and painting and sketches on the back burner for her husband and daughter and hadn't given it a second thought. Until now.

A war of emotions begins to build. Peggy throws the shirt down, stares at it with hate in her tear- filled eyes. She grabs it and begins ripping and tearing the shirt, wishing it is her husband, instead of only his shirt.

Recognition comes to her as the threads give way, it is the smell of the perfume. She stops, startled at the realization. She knows the scent, smells it regularly. Another wave of angry hurt washes over her. It is the perfume her new best friend wears.

Peggy scrubs the smeared mascara from her face, and then calls her babysitter to see if she can come stay with Robin this evening. She dials Tammy's number and isn't surprised when there is no answer. She hates that, to have her suspicions confirmed. She goes back into the bathroom, reapplies her makeup and lays out some clean clothes. She is ready when the sitter arrives.

Peggy plays out the scenario in her mind while she drives toward town. She'll try going to her husband's work site first, and then she'll drive by the bars. She will find them. No matter what her mother told her, she is better than this. No one deserves being treated this way.

Peggy drives by the empty, half completed house he is working on, barely slowing down in case a worker is still around. She makes a U-turn and heads toward town. She pulls into the bar parking lot and doesn't see either of their cars. She pulls around the back and spots his truck. She decides this needs to be handled head on. She checks her lipstick in the rearview mirror before climbing out. Peggy takes a deep breath, pulls her shirttail down and pushes the back door open. She stands for a minute, allowing her eyes to adjust to the dark, noisy room. No one notices she has come in.

Through the haze she sees them, at a table in the corner. Jim is sitting with his back to the wall, his arm draped around Tammy while his other hand holds a bottle of beer. Tammy is snuggled up to Jim, looking up at him in adoration. Peggy turns and slips back out the door. When she slides into the car, she lays her head against the steering wheel and begins sobbing loudly. There is no denying what her own eyes saw. Her mother was right, she is a stupid fool.

Lori

Lori doesn't see her husband when he leans on the new fancy porch post and studies the building going on. Peggy's husband has gotten the job of building their new home. She doesn't see him when he is lost in thought. When he silently hopes this will make Lori finally happy. She had chosen the floor plan and had added all kinds of fancy things to the house plans. The new house will be finished within a month.

When they'd bought this piece from his granddaddy to build on, Lori had wrinkled up her newly altered nose. She thought five miles were quite a distance from town. Tommy promised to build her a new house, near the creek that babbled through the rolling hills. She had watched him repair the old barn, saw his love for the stout, moss covered oak boards. He respected the pioneer who made the barn and chose the setting, he tells her. The hills are covered with wildflowers and rich grass every spring. He has been working at putting the old ditches back into use for irrigation. He will make a show place, the new house set under the big trees on the hill, with the old orchard close by. He's put up an arena by the old rock corrals. But, Lori senses he is baffled by her actions. He doesn't understand her resistance to what he thinks of as a family place. As much as he loves her, he can't understand her.

Tommy tells her he can look at the green hill rolling down to the creek and picture two little kids playing beside it. A little girl with blonde curls sitting on the bank and a red headed boy wading in the water with his jeans rolled up. Just like he had done when he was little. When he asks Lori about starting a family, she tells him she isn't ready, maybe in a few years she might be. She knows he wonders why she always seems distant whenever he brings up the subject. Heck, he's even said he'll pay to have her looks brought back after having a baby, if that is what her problem is. She knows her looks aren't near as important to him as they are to her. He will do anything for Lori. She's just had her nose done and he hadn't thought there was a thing wrong with it. He just doesn't know what else he can do for her.

Lori enters the cool foyer and pulls off her expensive sunglasses. She kicks off her shoes and feels the cool stone on her feet. She stops at the gilt-framed mirror and studies her face. Damn squint lines are back. That high dollar cream only works so long. She knows time is moving forward and she dreads the thought of a total facelift in ten or fifteen years. She has to take care of herself, no matter what. She can't risk losing Tommy's, or any man's desire. She has her hands full avoiding Tommy's need-to-start-a-family soon subject. They are in their thirties now and, truthfully, she doesn't know if she'll ever be ready. There was a note on the refrigerator from Tommy, telling her to call someone back. Lori doesn't recognize the number. She pours herself a tall glass of sweet tea. She'll ask Tommy more about the call when he comes in. The housekeeper has left instructions for some casserole that must be in the refrigerator. It is too hot for that kind of country heavy food. Maybe she'll talk Tommy into going to the steakhouse again. She can have a salad and not have to worry about her weight. She really needs to talk to the housekeeper again. The last time she had tried to discuss the heavy food the woman pointed out to her that she felt Tommy needed real food. He is outside working every day, then works on the ranch when he gets home. Lori had felt the silent condemnation of the woman. Tommy is free to go eat wherever and whenever he wants. Lori isn't going to slave away over a hot stove, not when there are lots of choices. Lori hears Tommy come in, hears his boots on the stones of the entryway. She quickly pats her hair and pulls her stomach in before striking a pose against the counter. She makes sure to slightly lift her chin before she fixes her smile and widens her eyes. "You look about done in. Let me pour you some tea, sweetheart," she says, smiling even wider.

"That sounds really good," he replies as studies Lori's face. She is still pretty as a picture, he thinks, always looks so perfect.

"It is just too hot. I know I must look a sight. A girl can't even keep makeup on, it just slides off," she says as she dabs at her face. "Let's go grab something in town. Sheila left some ol' casserole, and it is just too hot to turn the oven on. Whatcha think, sugar?" she asks in her sweetest tone.

"Don't you want to call that gal back before we go? It will cool down a bit if we wait awhile."

"That's not a bad idea. You go sit down for a bit and rest and I'll go call her back from the study. What did she want? I forgot what you said."

"I'm not real sure, just call her and you'll find out," Tommy says tiredly as he takes his tea to the living room. Lori grabs the note and heads for the study. She recognizes the number as being from Oregon. On the third ring, a woman answers. Just a soft hello, no business name.

"Hi, I'm returning a call from someone at this number." Lori idly draws in the sweat on her glass while she waits for the woman to respond. This is kinda weird, she thinks.

"Is this Lori?" the young, almost girl-like voice asks.

"Yes, ma'am, it is. May I ask what this is about?" Lori responds firmly, quickly losing patience.

"The Lori who graduated in 1974, the cheerleader and rodeo queen?"

Lori considers where this is going. Maybe some young girl is going to do a story on her, probably about their life, Tommy's feed business, their good horses and their showcase home.

"Goodness, that was a while ago! Oh, yes, that's me" Lori answers sweetly. "What's this all about, sugar?" There is a moment of silence before the woman answers.

"I guess I am your daughter."

Lori looks around anxiously. She's over a hundred miles from home, someone she knows or Tommy knows might still see her. She chose an upscale place where she and Tommy had met some of his clients. When the waiter comes, she orders iced tea, though she feels like throwing up. The flowers on the table seem to smell too sweet, and the silverware has been lined up precisely and repeatedly. It shows smudges from her sweaty fingers.

Damn government anyway. Opening adoption records and making finding people who don't want to be found too easy. She is torn, doesn't know if she wants to see this child she gave birth to, or just get up and drive home, and pretend the phone call never happened. She looks down at her slim wrist, checks her expensive watch again. She doesn't see the hostess leading the young woman to her table.

Lori decides she will go. It is all probably a farce, someone thinking they'll get some money out of her, blackmail her. She begins to rise when the voice she recognizes from the phone speaks from beside her. Lori freezes and shuts her eyes.

The voice is like her Granny's, she realizes. And the face that goes with it is like the pictures she saw of her Granny when she was young. How'd she ever not recognize that voice on the phone? This is no game; this child has to be hers. Her baby. Oh, God.

The young woman smiles, a trembling smile as she seats herself across from Lori. Oh, no. Lori's heart seems to turn within her chest. The smile is Tommy's. She had always wondered, when she allowed herself to think about the baby she gave up. Now, she knows. Her husband is really the father.

Lori knows she's been acting as nervous as a long-tailed cat in a room full of rockers lately. Tommy can't figure out what is going on, and he knows better than to press her. Lori has no idea he's been paying bills and catching up the bank accounts while she was gone. No idea he saw the charges for meals and even a room when she'd told him she was going off to see her family. She doesn't have any family that lives there, at least that he knows of. Not any kind of kin, and he should know since their family lines crossed so many times.

Back in the old days small towns didn't give folks a big choice of who to marry. Most everyone was related in some way or another. She isn't there when he feels anger begin to burn when he thinks of her with someone else, eating fancy dinners, sharing a hotel room.

Tommy had stopped and gotten some roses, the fancy kind that came in their own crystal vase, hoping maybe that would make her happy. He'd finished the book work before he heard her driving in. Lori 's car pulls into the garage and the door opens into the utility room. She appears, and smiles when she sees Tommy. He catches a glimpse of the worried frown she replaces with a smile. Lori walks over to him for a hug and comments on how beautiful the flowers are, and how she doesn't deserve a man like Tommy. Lori doesn't notice the lack of reply or reaction from Tommy.

After a somewhat strained dinner, Lori asks Tommy to sit out on the porch with her and have another glass of wine. Tommy fills their glasses and settles next to his wife on the big swing. The view is beautiful, the sun turning the rolling hills into a gold tinted green where the horses are grazing. Down by the creek some of the Longhorns are resting and chewing their cud contentedly. Lori feels his pride of the place, and remembers how he says it sometimes felt like it is a dream. In his eyes, the skinny Okie kid had made it big. His daddy would have been so proud, he'd tell her.

Lori reaches for Tommy's hand and looks into his

eyes. Her lip quivers as she begins to speak.

"I have to tell you something, and hope you can find it in your heart to forgive me. You mean everything to me, and I can't imagine being without you." Tommy keeps his face stiff while he feels his heart sink. Damn it, he is right. He will kill the SOB.

Lori sees hurt and anger in his face. She gently grabs his chin and tells him to look at her. "It's not what you think. I am not seeing anyone else. You will always be the only one for me." Lori sips her wine to give her courage before she begins speaking.

"Do you remember right after high school when I went away? To work for an aunt? That isn't why I went away. I was pregnant. Pregnant, Tommy. I had the baby, a girl, and gave it up for adoption. It was all set up. She went to a great home, the folks adopting her were respected and successful. I know you always wanted us to have a baby, and this is one reason why I wouldn't try to get pregnant. I just couldn't. I couldn't try to have a child when I already had one out there. I hope you can try to understand. Anyway, she called me and we have been meeting. I am so sorry I didn't tell you about her years ago, I just never thought I'd ever see her. I know you need time to digest this, and hope someday you can forgive me for keeping this from you."

A fat tear slowly slides down Lori's carefully made up face. She can see he is shocked. All these years when he was wanting, aching really, for a child. She already had one and he had no idea.. Tommy looks up when Lori clears her throat.

"Tommy, you have to believe me, I never meant to hurt you this way. Every time you'd hint at us having a baby, I'd want to tell you I wish we could have one. Oh, God. They said I couldn't ever have another. I couldn't let you find out the reason I couldn't have a baby or that I already had a child."

Tommy interrupts her, his voice like a knife as he tells her she chose to lie to him for all these years. He repeats she did have a choice, and she had chosen the wrong one. What the hell, she was lying all these years by keeping this secret. He stares at his wife. A woman he no longer knows, he tells Lori. Who knows what else she is lying about?

"Tommy, I know you are angry, and you are hurting. There's something else you need to know. You are the father. We have a child, a beautiful daughter. There's no doubt she is yours, wait til you see her."

Tommy stares at his wife. He grips the wine glass until the stem breaks. He doesn't see the blood running out between his fingers. Then something happens, something snaps in Lori. Tommy is startled, he's never seen her look like this. She suddenly jumps up and yells in his face that she is a whore. She always had been and always will be. She hurries off the porch and starts running down the lane, tearing at her clothes. Tommy jumps in his truck and chases her down, finally pulling in front of her to try and stop her. She is almost to the road with most of her dress ripped off and cars are beginning to honk at the wild semi-nude woman. He grabs her while she begins screaming for everyone to stop and see the whore. He picks her up and throws her in the pickup while she beats him with her fists. He can see blood on her chest and shoulders where she's violently tried to rip off her clothes.

PART FIVE

When the Chickens Come Home to Roost

Deanna Dickinson McCall

Chapter Nineteen

Peggy

Peggy watches the young girl warming up her horse. She and her husband sit on their horses at the end of the arena. He reaches over and squeezes her hand. Jim takes every opportunity he can find to make Peggy feel loved. He still felt so much guilt for hurting her.

"She's so much like you, watching her is like stepping back in time." He smiles tenderly at Peggy and squeezes her hand again.

Peggy returns his squeeze and tells him the child she had named Robin was a combination of them both, the best of them, she hopes. She also feels secure in the knowledge that Robin knows her parents love her.

Robin always tries her best and wants to please her parents but is allowed to make mistakes that are quickly forgiven. Peggy and Jim just want her to have the opportunity to learn from them, but then leave them behind as children should do.

The sound of a truck and trailer slowing down to turn into the lane announce Mike's arrival. Peggy hopes her mother hasn't come with him. Mike loves riding with Robin, and enjoys being part of her life, especially the horse part. He also loves roping with her, always giving her pointers and tips. Mike makes a stellar granddaddy. Sandy is still the disapproving witch, though not as bad with Robin as she had been with Peggy.

Peggy thought of the wall of buckles in the house and the trophy saddles sitting beside that wall. Robin has added to both the wall and saddle display, and she has done it without being told she was never good enough. Simple loving encouragement coupled with natural talent has proven to be a winning formula. Peggy would be just as proud of her daughter if she hadn't chosen to continue in her family's legacy of horses and rodeo. Robin has also placed in the local fair's art show. Peggy loved it when they were attending the awards and Sandy's friend told Sandy she was so fortunate to have both her daughter and granddaughter be so talented. The smile Sandy gave in return was painful, more of a grimace.

Suzy

Suzy stares at her kids. Her head is pounding, and she can't believe they'd dare give her lip. It is Ronnie's fault. She should never have married him, shouldn't have fallen for his gold buckle dreams, his fancy flashy ways. Now, she has two Ronnie clones to handle. Two people full of themselves, in her opinion. Thank God Ronnie is only here when he picks up or returns the damn brats. Sometimes she wonders if she should have tried harder with Ronnie. She just can't tolerate his straight-laced, holier than thou ways.

"You talk to me like that again, you won't have all your teeth" she snarls. "I sure as hell didn't raise you to talk to your elders like that. Of all the stupid things, talking to your mother like that," her voice is as sharp as a knife.

The teenagers stare at her. The girl finally speaks up. "Maybe if you acted with respect you'd get treated that way. Instead of like some old trampy Okie has-been, hanging out at the bars and everything." The girl's brother stares wide- eyed at his sister. While he might be been thinking along those lines, he would never voice those thoughts. His daddy has told him to just play along and when Suzy passes out to go do what he wanted to do. His dad laughed hard and added it has always worked for him.

"Even granddaddy said he was ashamed at your

'carrying on', that's what he called it. Grandmother said she'd call it catting around. I know why dad left, he couldn't take any more of your drinking and hanging out at the bars. Bet you didn't know we know all about you. And that you've done more than just drinking, too!" The girl held her ground, though her lip quivers and her eyes are bright with tears.

Suzy stares at the child, a mirror image of herself years ago. Little witch, she thinks. Not gonna pull that goody two-shoes crap on her. Suzy shifts her gaze to her son, sixteen months older than her daughter. He is the spittin' image of Ronnie, except he is usually a quiet, humble kid. Maybe she'll go to the bar and get away from this crap. Her kids are as bad as what her damn folks used to accuse Suzy of being, always full of lip and accusations. Hell, Suzy acting awful is the only thing her brother and her parents have ever agreed on.

Chapter Twenty

Donna

Donna stares at the papers in her hand and doesn't respond to the doctor's question until he asks it a second time. She slowly shakes her head. There is no one to call. He tells her to stop by the desk on her way out, that he has paperwork waiting for her. She numbly nods and grabs her purse. The nurse follows her, gently stopping her at the desk. She places the brochures and papers in a plastic bag and gives them to Donna. She gives Donna a hug and steps back. Donna tries to acknowledge the simple act of kindness without totally losing it and bawling. She nods slightly and heads for the door.

Donna climbs into the pickup and heads for her place. The countryside she is driving through is a blur. She pulls off the road, drives through her gate and parks near the barn. One of the mules looks up and shakes its head at her. She unlatches the gate and it comes to her, laying its big head against her chest. She sobs against the warmth, wrapping her arms around his head. "You might be sad they are going. I am not." Donna blubbers. "These big boobs have caused me more pain in my life than anything." Donna steps back and wipes her tears. Her shoulders ache even now. Perhaps the diagnosis of breast cancer can have a sort of twisted good outcome.

Donna goes to meet the team assigned to her, aids, nurses and doctors. When she tells them a mastectomy is what she wants, they reluctantly agree that would be wise, but warn her chemo and radiation will also be needed. Surgery is scheduled, to be followed with chemo and radiation, dependent upon the biopsy results. Donna tells no one of the diagnosis or treatment plan. She will get through this like she has everything in life, alone. She will figure it out.

The knocking on the door startles Donna. She had finally fallen asleep and starts to jump up, only to moan in pain. She hears a woman's voice, saying she is coming in. Donna tries to roll slightly to her side, maybe she can use an elbow to help herself sit up.

Footsteps come down the hall. Who is coming and why? She tries again to figure a way to sit up. A face appears in the bedroom doorway, it is a cousin she hasn't seen in decades. One from her long-gone mama's side. "Kelly? Is that you? What are you doing here?" Donna feels slightly dizzy and tries to focus.

"I tried calling you when I found out you were living here. I came by a couple of times and the neighbors said they'd been doing your chores while you went somewhere." Kelly stares at Donna and slowly approaches the bed. "What on earth has happened to you, Donna? I thought your neighbors said you were traveling or something. Are you all right? You aren't on drugs or something, are you?"

Donna's mouth feels like it is full of cotton. She tries to reach for the bottle of water she asked the driver to place on the nightstand. She grimaces and her cousin grabs the bottle and hands it to her. "Let me help you, honey."

Kelly sees the bandages beneath the sheets. "Why is your chest all bandaged up, Donna? Lord, girl, I sure never expected to walk into this! You didn't have a boob job, did you? You inherited all of our grandmother's and your mama's bounty there, I sure wouldn't have thought you'd wanted to add on to that."

Donna manages to swallow some water and leans back carefully. The surgeon told her she wasn't to lay flat down, and she is sore from laying in an unfamiliar position for so long. "Yeah, I just got out of the hospital, Kelly. I had Grandmother's legacy cut down, I sure didn't add to it. I'll be all right, I'm just sore from laying in one place so long."

"Well, I guess this is a good lesson for me not to just pop in on folks. I'm sorry, I just found out last week you were living here. Shoot, we all thought you were still living in California. I was awful sorry to hear about your daddy, despite everything that went on with your mama and him. Guess that wife of his didn't want anyone to know in time to go out there for his funeral."

Donna nods. "Yeah, she didn't even let me know my daddy was sick 'til it was too late. I made it to the service and that was it. I've been out of California for quite a while now." Donna stares at her cousin, her mama's sister's child. They'd come out a couple of times while Donna was growing up and hadn't stayed long. Donna's stepmom made sure they knew they really weren't welcome, so they'd end up staying at Gail's most of the time. Gail's family and both Donna's daddy and mama's families had been friends and neighbors in Oklahoma.

"Can I do anything for you, honey? I know you aren't up for company right now. I will come back when you're feeling better. I guess you got a nurse or someone coming in to help you, so I am gonna get out of your hair, now. I am fixing to put my number on the ice box so when you feel better you can call and we'll visit."

Donna manages to smile and nod. "That'll be great, Kelly. I'll look forward to that. Sorry I am not fit for company, thanks for coming, anyway. We'll catch up later." Donna closes her eyes and tries to fall back into a world where the pain floated away.

Peggy

Peggy stands in the foyer, nervously twisting the fetish strands carved of turquoise and other stones hanging about her neck. The gray stones match the threads in her hair. She's earned every single gray strand. Five more minutes and the gallery will open. She's watched the caterers setting up, the linen tablecloths draping gracefully into puddles on the carpet, the fine crystal champagne flutes and the china and silver plates filled with delicacies. Her daddy would say she was in high cotton, her mother would be looking critically down her long nose, trying to find fault with something. She didn't invite her parents. Inviting her daddy was impossible without including her mother. Her daughter and son-in-law would arrive shortly. That meant so much to her. She feels her confidence rise as she remembers them sharing the news with everyone.

She feels a tear begin as she thinks of her husband and how proud he would have been to be here. He insisted she continue painting when he was diagnosed with cancer, to not let his illness stop her. She really owes tonight to him. He believed in her when no one did, made her finally understand she was worthy, she was talented, despite the hell even he had put her through. She misses him not being here with her, especially tonight. She prays every day that the chemo and radiation will work. She had been enraged when her mother hinted that Jim's cancer might be God's answer to his cheating on Peggy. Peggy ordered her out of her house and said things she should have said long ago. It was a long-needed cleansing for Peggy to say those things out loud.

Peggy looks around and still can't believe she is here, that her paintings are hanging in this world-famous gallery and that she is having this solo artist show. She's been told movie stars, politicians, and other famous folks will be there. The portraits she's painted of animals and western scenes, along with some landscapes lined the walls, in beautiful frames. A couple approach her with press badges hanging around their necks. They introduce themselves and announce they are covering the opening for Art of The West magazine. The man's badge says his name is Jacque, and when he sees Peggy reading it, he tells her it is pronounced with the French pronunciation. Like Peggy wouldn't know that. They ask her to step into a side room for a quick interview.

The questions begin, where the inspiration comes from. She explains she grew up in a little town almost 200 miles north of the Bay area. She sees the reporters exchange glances when she answers their question of which town. "A real cow town, with a reputation to match." Something city folks don't understand. They asked how she was ever exposed to the art world. Did her parents bring her here or to L.A. to experience real art? Peggy takes a deep breath before answering them. She explains she was fortunate enough to have everyday interaction with the animals, cowboys, rodeo, and ranch life she portrays in her work. She grew up where art was respected, and if it was cowboy art, it had better be 100% accurate in detail and subject, she points out.

Jacque looks doubtful when he repeats her answer that the little town and its people had taught her so much. She bites her tongue, assures him that is exactly what she means. She is relieved when the curator comes to get her, telling her the doors are about to open and Peggy is needed to stand in the place of honor. She politely excuses herself and breaths a sigh of relief to be away from the clueless reporters.

Sandy glares at Peggy and thumps her cane on the floor. "Keep that damn cat away from me. I know good and well that filthy thing is waiting for me to fall asleep so it can smother me, just like it did my baby!" Jim watches his mother-in-law, shaking his head in disapproval at her. Sometimes Jim could reason with her, and she'd listen.

Peggy cringes. She's learned a lot of things as her mother's dementia progresses, things that came out and were never mentioned before. Peggy thought they were just figments of her mother's imagination until the doctor told her things mentioned in the past are often true things that they remember, and admitted that occasionally old secrets come out. Peggy had gone to the courthouse and looked up records when Sandy kept asking about her baby named Tammy. Peggy discovered Tammy had been almost two years older than Peggy. She had been found dead in her crib not long after Peggy was born. The thought of having had a sister makes her ache. Peggy never knew about the baby, but she had always dreamed of having a sister, someone to giggle with, ride with, and to divert some of her mother's scalding remarks. Maybe some part of her knew she did have a sister. Peggy talked to some of her mother's oldest friends and got them to open up to her. She learned Sandy had blamed herself, and then Peggy for Tammy's death. Sandy felt she had been too worried about the new baby and hadn't paid enough attention to Tammy, reasoning in her twisted way that if Peggy hadn't been born, she'd still have her first born. The child who looked more like Sandy and not like Mike's Indian looking family.

Peggy feels the resentment rise again that Mike had passed away first and left Peggy to take care of Sandy. Age has not improved the bitter woman. Peggy feels a pang of guilt as she thinks about the child her mother lost. She can't imagine losing a child. Maybe it helps explain in some small way her mother's unhappiness all these years. It still is so wrong and hurtful to blame Peggy for that loss, she knows that. Peggy just continues praying she never becomes the angry hateful woman her mother is.

Peggy also knows for her own sanity, she will have to place Sandy in a home soon. Caring for both Jim and her mother is exhausting, and she needs time to paint. Her paintings cover many extra expenses, including the woman she hires to come in and watch Sandy while Peggy paints in the studio. Sandy had thrown the soup the woman had served her, scalding the woman's face. Peggy doesn't blame the woman for leaving and not coming back. Jim tries to help and while he is regaining some strength he can't care for his mother-in-law. Peggy knows the time has come to make the decision.

Peggy flips the long braid over her shoulder. It is shot with silver now, and hangs to her waist. She adjusts the oxygen flow on the machine and smiles up at her husband. "That better, Jim?" She has managed to appear calm and matter-of-fact when she looks up. She was painting in the corner of her studio when she heard the beeper go off. It always causes her to panic, and she hurried out to the living room. Jim had smiled when she came running, telling her he was sorry, he should have been paying attention. She worries about him and she knows he feels he doesn't deserve her love and care, he has told her that. Peggy hates him being tied to the damn machine probably as much as he does, and prays it won't be forever. The doctors think he might be able to gradually be weaned off of it during the day. His own construction crew had come and put safety handles in the bathrooms. They'd also made a ramp to the front door so Peggy could push him in the wheelchair when he'd not even been able to stand.

Peggy studies her husband. His face is still ash colored and she can see the bones of his knees under his jeans. His hair has begun to grow back and is like the down on a baby duck, soft and fine. The lines in his face have grown deeper with the weight loss. When she'd sit by him holding his hand for hours and hours while chills and nausea overtook him from the chemo, he had begged and begged her for forgiveness. She'd reassure him time and time again that the past was the past. The age gap between Peggy and Jim has become more obvious with his illness.

"Oh, honey, what hurts?" Peggy kneels down and kisses the age spotted hand wrapped around hers. She is so thankful she still has him, it makes her heart hurt to know that someday one of them will be alone.

Chapter Twenty-One

Suzy

The woman's hands are plump, and the diamonds circling them match the ones sparkling from her ears. She lifts a heavy arm to push the gray/blonde hair back away from her face again, and then climbs down the bleachers. Her shorts show her thick thighs tapering down to tiny ankles that disappear into fancy fringed moccasins. Once she reaches the bottom, her belly leads the way. She is going after another corn dog, and maybe a fried Twinkie. She looks at the beer stand as she passes it.

"Hey, Suzy!" She turns to see Tommy, and breaks into a wide smile. "I thought that was you. Where ya been keeping yourself, gal?" He still has his crooked grin, though wrinkles frame it and there is silver showing at his temples below his hat.

Suzy gives him a hug, and knows Tommy realizes how much bigger she is. He always said she was built like a football player. He is thinking like a retired one, now. He steps back and looks at her. It has been at least 10 years since he's seen her, and life hasn't been kind. Suzy knows that. She hates that her hard living is etched in her face.

"I came to watch my nephew. He's been doing good, and I helped get him a really good horse. That's what rich aunt's do, isn't it?" she laughs, then adds she didn't ride any more, though both of her kids still ride, and her daughter and son often rope together.

"How's Ronnie doing? Must be good, if you all are rich." Tommy says jokingly.

Suzy is startled at the question. She figured Tommy knew. "Tommy, we haven't been together for a long time. The kids still see him, of course. I honestly don't know how he is. I am with someone else now." She pauses a moment before continuing, "I know you won't ask. I've been off the stuff for over ten years, that's why I am bigger than my mama!" she giggles. "My new husband treats me really good, spoils me, really. It beats the hell outta getting knocked around, like the last one I had. Yep, I'm on number three husband. And this one doesn't want me working, he makes lots of money. So, I can do what I want, eat what I want. I just can't do drugs or drink, or be with the old bad folks I used to hang out with, that's the only rules."

"Well, I am happy for you, gal. Glad you got your life back on track, glad you seem to have found someone to have a life with, and happy you're getting along with your family again. At least, I figure you are, if you're buying nephews good horses!"

Suzy smiles, and tells him thanks, and gives him one more hug, telling him that one is for Lori. She didn't ask how Lori was, she realizes as she marches past the beer stand. Tommy shakes his head as he watches her make her way toward the bleachers, carrying a corn dog, cotton candy and caramel corn.

Suzy reads the newspapers and keeps current with the local rodeo news. When she hears of someone needing a helping hand, she anonymously sends them cash. Sometimes it is a big amount, dependent on need. It might be to help with medical bills, a kid needing a new horse or someone needing a new start. Suzy drove a hundred to two hundred miles once a month to mail the cash so no one would ever know where it came from. The driving also helps the need she still feels to be on the road, one habit leftover from rodeo she still hasn't shaken.

Suzy smiles at the woman behind the counter.

She'd seen the woman's thinly veiled reaction when Suzy told her how much cash she wanted. Then she watched when the woman pulled up Suzy's account. The woman has a hard time hiding her shock. She pushes a button under the counter to have the bank manager appear. He smiles and asked Suzy how she was while nodding it was all right at the teller.

"Yes, ma'am, I want it all in one hundred-dollar bills. I know it is a lot, you can put it in this bank bag here." Suzy pushes the bag toward her and tries to be patient with the middle age woman, but she can feel the woman's jealousy like a cold wind circling around her. Suzy started banking at this place a few months ago, opening a couple of accounts. She'd always banked in the little local bank, but she doesn't always like those folks knowing everything she does. She'd grown up and gone to school with about every teller and the manager there. Suzy needs some privacy sometimes.

Suzy pulls the car over to a corner of the parking lot under a tree. She locks the doors and makes sure her pistol is where she can reach it. She pulls the bills out and begins placing the stacks of money into envelopes. Her husband doesn't care what she does with her money, or really what she does period, as long as she doesn't bring any of the "damn goat roper bunch" around him. He has made it plain that he wants no part of Suzy's old life to be revived and brought home. He didn't care when she told him she was buying horses for her kids and nephew. Just don't bring those "damned red-necked people" home to him was his only comment.

She licks the last envelope and looks around carefully before starting the car. She thinks of her family. When her brother was hurt and wouldn't accept her help, she'd even sent him cash anonymously. She's bought his son the best horse she could find. He did let her do that. It had taken awhile for him to come around, to realize his sister was genuinely sorry. Sorry for the way he had been overlooked while they were growing up, sorry for so many things.

The coffee has grown cold and bitter and Suzy puts the cup back down. She looks at the clock and is surprised to see an hour has passed. Passed and gone, to never return. Like so much of her life, like so many people in her life. She ignores the ringing phone that has interrupted her thoughts. He probably won't even bother coming home before going to the office, much less call, she thinks. She pushes up from the table leaving the phone unanswered and looks around at the house. It has everything a person could want, every convenience, decorated in a modern style, all chrome and glass. Nothing to make it a home, no softening of pillows, afghans, drapes or even a book on a table. Cold and impersonal, a reflection of him she realizes. When

Suzy mentioned getting some throw pillows and drapes, he had stared at her, telling her he had paid big money for the designer to get the house to look like it does.

She doesn't know how much longer she can take living like this. She puts on a good front, telling her old friends how good she has it, while rarely accepting invitations to do things with them and never being able to invite them over. He had told her he didn't want any of her old trashy people around, though he hadn't said it quite that way in the beginning, the message was clear. She can go see her brother, watch her nephew and go visit her kids. He prefers she go there for holidays, he doesn't need the headache of having "these people" around. She is surprised he hadn't wanted it all in writing.

He'd gone on another business trip to New York and she had stayed home, as usual. She is bored with the picture-perfect wives that would be there. She thinks of their designer clothes, expensive scents and perfect faces and looks down at her belly. Better this than drugs or booze she thinks as she grabs a cinnamon roll to put in the microwave.

The automated voice of the security system tells her the microwave is done heating and someone is approaching her front door. She hates the voice and its continual drone of what is happening in the house and other stupid news. If it knew so damn much why didn't it tell the microwave to not turn on before food was really hot, and tell her to quit eating, she thought to herself as she walks to the door. She is puzzled to see someone from her husband's office standing there. The woman is attractive and smiles nervously as Suzy opens the door. "Hi, I'm Sharon, I don't know if you remember me, I'm from the office." Suzy notes the revealing neckline of the woman's blouse before stepping back to let her enter. The woman shakes her head slightly and reaches in her briefcase to hand Suzy a large envelope. The secretary looks at Suzy quickly before smirking and announcing, "You've been served, dear" and turns on her heel to walk away. Suzy slowly closes the door and tells the voice announcing the front door was closed to shut the hell up while she rips open the envelope.

He has filed for divorce and wants her out of his house within 24 hours.

Lori

Lori watches Wynonna's face, shiny with sweat as she grimaces and grabs Lori's hand even tighter. Lori cringes and tells herself no way would she ever go through all this natural childbirth stuff. It was bad enough when she had Wynonna and she had even had a spinal block. Lori remembered little of giving birth, she was advised to forget the experience along with the baby and go on with life. She hasn't been able to completely do that. The memory of the baby she barely got to see returned to taunt her from time to time throughout the years. Sometimes she could keep the image pushed away, but when Tommy talked about starting a family it always surfaced and terrified her. The fear of the secret coming out was so awful. She realized she felt relief when Wynonna finally found her and everything came out in the open. The only thing that ever worries her is the fact she and Tommy are kin. It was several generations back, and in like most small-towns, everyone back there was related in one way or another. Wynonna's DNA test confirmed Lori and Tommy shared DNA, though it was a tiny, tiny amount.

Lori wonders if part of the difficulty of her daughter giving birth is the possibility of Wynonna missing the woman who raised her. Her real mother, Lori reminds herself. Lori wasn't part of that and couldn't pretend she was. Lori hates the fact that woman and her husband gave Wynonna an ultimatum, that if Wynonna is going to allow Lori and Tommy into her life they are done with her.

Wynonna told Lori about the conversation she overheard. "For heaven's sake, her birth parents were married to each other and never tried to find Wynonna? What kind of people do that, and Wynonna was going to welcome them into her life?" It was more than they could understand. Lori knows they are probably deeply hurt and suggests she try to talk to them. To explain that it isn't her or Tommy's intention to replace them. Wynonna told her it would only make things worse if Lori tried to reason with them.

Lori wipes her daughter's brow and as she bent down to kiss her cheek a tear falls, startling Wynonna. She smiles and tells Lori it is okay. She is glad Lori is here. She can't imagine what it had been like for Lori to give birth, a teenager all alone with no mother, knowing that she'd never see the child she was giving birth to.

The doctor tells Wynonna the baby is coming and as she gives a huge push, Lori watches her grandchild enter the world. The child the doctor held in his arms is silent and Lori tries to give her daughter a reassuring look while she fights down her own fears. Oh, Lord, she prays, please make everything be okay. The doctor smiles and announces it is a girl before turning the baby over and tapping her on her back. The baby begins to hiccup and cry. The baby is placed on its mother's breast and Lori looks on in awe, tears streaming. She now knows the very beginning of what she has missed. She'll be damned if those ignorant people will keep her from this baby, she decides. She has had enough of trying to please folks, she'd done it all her life and it didn't work.

Lori sees Tommy standing on the patio and watching the children playing along the creek below. She watches as he cocks his head to listen to her and their daughter talking inside. Their daughter. Sometimes, it is still hard for Tommy and Lori both to absorb that word. Those are their grandchildren playing below. She wonders if he thinks back to all the times that he has stood on this spot and imagined his own children playing on that creek. She knows that sometimes he is torn, so sad they have missed Wynonna's childhood. Other times, he tells her he is just so thankful he has these kids in his life. That it makes his heart swell just looking at them.

Lori feared he would blame her for missing so much of their daughter's life, and he actually had for a while. He had blown up at Lori. When he finally listened, he understood his wife a bit more. Though it had almost killed Lori, she finally told him she didn't think he was the father, she was pretty sure it was the good-for-nothin' boyfriend who left town. After all, Tommy and Lori only slept together that one time, when he was comforting her, trying to tell her she was a great gal and the boyfriend was a conceited, self-centered jerk. That it was good riddance the boyfriend had been practically run out of town. God, they were both kids back then and let things get out of hand. Hugs and sweet kisses meant to comfort turned into something else that night.

Then, years later, when Wynonna found them, Lori had been typical Lori. She didn't want folks to know she'd given away a baby years ago, especially since it was Tommy's child, too. She just knew folks would be saying she gave up the child because she was afraid it wouldn't be right, with her and Tommy being related way back. And Lori couldn't defend that very well by admitting she thought someone else was the father. It was the one time Tommy put his foot down. He'd sat her down and told her he was done with worrying about what folks thought. He finally had a family and he was damned proud of them. He planned on taking Wynonna with them to all the local places and he'd introduce her as their daughter. People could be damned. He made Lori laugh when he said folks would know she was their daughter the minute they saw her, she was the best-looking woman in the state. How could any child of theirs be anything but perfect?

Lori knew that Tommy knew he had hurt her

deeply. He'd made her go to counseling after she lost it that world-changing evening several years ago. He had shuddered at the recollection of Lori a few years ago. Eyes wild, clothes shredded and calling herself a whore. He'd even gone with her to see the therapist when she asked him to come. He'd tried to explain he never meant to hurt her. That he would always love and respect his wife. Tommy told her he wondered how much trust Lori had left for him.

Lori stares at her reflection in the mirror. She sees what Wynonna sees for the first time, a woman who looks preserved. That is the perfect word. Leave it to her daughter, the writer. Lori doesn't know where that talent has come from. Wynonna laughed when her mother said that, asking her if she didn't realize both Tommy and Lori's family were born storytellers. Lori told Tommy what Wynonna said and he has pondered it. He tells Lori she is right, they come from country people who share family histories and stories. Both of them and almost everyone they grew up with has been raised that way. Though many of the family stories omit the hard years of the Dust Bowl. Tommy didn't know until a few years ago just how bad it had been for his granddaddy and daddy. They camped and found work where they could, often sleeping in ditches and going hungry. He didn't know the full extent they were looked down upon and called names, either. His uncle told him things his own daddy hadn't.

Lori makes the decision of no more surgeries and treatments. Tommy has told her for years she is beautiful and that God and nature knew far more about real beauty than any plastic surgeon. It makes Lori feel free since she reconciled herself to looking natural, like the grandmother she is. Lori wants to set an example for her daughter and granddaughter that looks are not the most important thing. Lori knows her own mama had raised her with the idea that looks were the most important thing with the best of intentions. She believed it was the only way she could help her daughter be successful in life.

Tommy has teased her about the streaks of silver in "Granny L's" hair; he loves to call her Granny L. Lori was filled with emotion the first time one of the grandchildren had come running in the house calling out for their Granny L. She had to swallow tears before she could answer them. She will never forget that day. Now those kids are growing up and Tommy has set up college funds for them and they've both had their wills changed to include them. She and Tommy are so proud of them and Wynonna.

Lori has begun to learn to not worry about what other folks thought. Her family is all that matters. She has even started a group to help adoptees and their parents reconnect, funded by her. She stood up at the first meeting and told the story of Tommy and her and the wonderful family she has now.

Chapter Twenty-Two

Me

A tear rolls down my face as I look over the desert. This will be the last day on this place. It is where my daughter and son grew up. It is where I gave up so much, believing I was making the right decisions by staying on what used to be called a rawhide place, not much more than a cow camp. No power, no phones, sixty-five miles to a loaf of bread. The blue mountains look like they should be on the edge of a frigid ocean rather than a sagebrush sea. It is a remote sort of beauty here, one I have learned to appreciate gradually. Buster and I are tired of the cold, tired of growing hay for six months to spend the next six throwing it at cattle. Starting over at our age won't be easy. But, I know it can't be much harder than what we've been through. Too many years of drought, extreme winters. Living hand to mouth, and working harder than anyone I ever knew. Our son doesn't love this life. He left to become a mechanical engineer. Guess the old tractors and hay equipment we can barely afford made him want better designs. Our daughter is younger, and has always loved the horses, and the old ways. She will move with us to be where our family came from a couple of generations ago.

We thought of going back to California, but all the reasons we left it are magnified now. It just got worse and worse. We will always need to have cows and horses. It is in my DNA, at least. We feel the tug of older roots. Twisted roots, some might think. We decide to go back to the country our grandparents and parents left. They were seeking a better life, and we are too. I wonder what they'd think knowing their children and grandchildren are returning to the land and culture they left.

I look at the trailers loaded and waiting. Stock trailers full of boxes and a few family antiques. We decide moving most of our furniture isn't feasible. It will be easier to buy new and makes more sense. We do pack my father-in-law's highchair. The story surrounding it will forever be carried in my family, I hope. It came across Route 66, tied onto an old car that stopped at every cotton camp for work and was often the only furniture in the tents the family stayed in. One time my father-in-law was tied into the chair to keep him safe in their canvas tent. His mother went after water, leaving him in the chair. Somehow, the chair fell over, onto the dog who always laid close hoping for a rare scrap to fall. The dog became frantic being penned under the chair and bit the child repeatedly. My father-in-law carried the scars and a misshapen finger the rest of his life.

The flat bed trailers are loaded down with a poor rancher's equipment and tools. Our saddles, along with some heirloom tack are stacked in the pickup back seats. The old Navajo and Hopi blankets that belonged to my grandfather are there, too.

We found a place that called to us. It was a place we both felt waited for us. A place we are supposed to be on. The minute we found it we somehow knew we had found home. We saw possibilities. It would take work, but we could do it. We could still run cattle and I would have my own nursery. I would finally be able to grow something without the extreme temperatures and seasons of the high desert. My love of growing things had been put on hold for decades in the fifty-five-day growing season of the old ranch. We could only grow alfalfa and grass, a necessity for stock.

Too cold to grow flowers for the soul, or fresh produce for our bellies.

I smile when I think of the yes ma'ams and no sirs

that are still so much part of life where we are going. Where church and God are still a priority and spoken about freely. I envision the green house and gardens we will build. I lift my chin and wish this valley a silent best of luck, and pray the one thing we leave behind is Buster's alcoholism.

I admire the new pens and loading chute we have built as I watch the last cow climb into the truck, and the door slide down. One less thing to worry about. I need to go to the house and make some calls. The native shrubs I ordered haven't arrived, and I have planned on having them for the big sale this weekend. I look down at my hands, they're pretty rough. I can hear my dad telling me they look like I'd been picking cotton. The memory brings a smile. So much of what he and my grandparents said and did rubbed off on me. So much more than I realized. One of the last cows to be loaded was black, a wild thing with spots on her face. I told the driver to watch the motley faced cow, and he stared at me before asking if I meant the brockled face. He was from up north and was also confused when I told him we'd break off and have dinner before continuing the loading this afternoon. I finally said lunch and I guess a light came on, from the look on his face.

My daughter has left a message. She has to travel off the mountain to get service for her phone. I know it must be important for her to call. She's running dude rides from a remote camp during the summer and on weekends, whenever she isn't in school. The message tells me she is coming home this weekend. I wonder why, what she is going to tell us. Quitting school, pregnant, not doing the rides or what? Guess we will find out in a couple of days. I've learned to not stress so much about what I can't change. At least I tell myself that.

Que sera, que sera.

I hear the door slam and Buster kicking his manure-covered boots off. He has finally learned after twenty-five years of marriage. Thank God for that. I call the nursery and track down the problem with the shrubs. I will start first thing in the morning on setting up the displays for the sale. Buster will be on his own, as far as ranch work is concerned. I think my ag. teachers would not be surprised that I couldn't decide between plants and cows and ended up with both. They might be surprised that I left and didn't look back. I found home, and it wasn't the desert I grew to love, and it wasn't where I came from. It was where some of my and Buster's people had come from.

I look around and sigh. We have built the place into a nice little ranch. It wasn't much when we bought the place. I feel pride, but also sadness that there is no one to pass it to. Our daughter decided she's had enough of rough living and is moving to the city. I doubt she will ever have children. The move shocked even me. She's grown up loving the ranch life and we've always pictured expanding the place to include her and whatever family she'd eventually have. Buster says he saw it coming. There were too many options out there other than to work as hard as we did and still do. Our son knew that the hard work on a ranch wasn't for him at an early age. The days of family ranches and farms are over, at least for my family and me.

I smile when I see one of the Longhorns Buster has turned into a pet come up for a treat of cake. I remember my daddy back in the eighties looking at the Longhorn crosses he'd bought and shaking his head, saying his granddaddy had spent all his life trying to breed the Longhorn out of his cows and now here he was with exactly the opposite. The memory revives the ache of missing the old family who instilled the never give up attitude and work ethic I still carry today.

The greenhouses are behind the hay and horse barns and I begin walking back to them. The flowers and trees we planted shelter the place, provide shade and protection from the Texas wind. The neighbors call our place the *Garden of Eden* or the *Oasis*. They are good people, like the folks we grew up with before rural California filled up with city folks wanting to move to what they called God's Country, gradually changing it into what they left. Buster and I have made a life here and are accepted as part of the community, unlike some of the new folks from California moving here. Having family ties here, despite it being from generations ago, sure helps. We've both met distant cousins. I wonder what our folks would think about us leaving California. It was The Promised land for them. I reflect on the sacrifices and struggles our families made to get there.

I stop by the hay barn to tell Buster I'm going to the greenhouse to check on things. The door is open, and I don't see him. I remember I need to take a wrench to tighten a waterline I noticed dripping and walk towards the shop. I pull open the doors and start toward the back wall where he keeps the hand tools. The smell of beer hits me in the face. I feel my heart sink and am filled with anger. Damn him all to hell. I begin looking for the stash. He's always hidden his beer and there was a time he even hid wine in the shops and barns. I can't find any cans or bottles, and yet I can't deny the smell, either. I will have to go back to watching, to find it before confronting him. I am sure he will use our daughter's decision to not be involved with the place as his excuse. He will use anything as an excuse.

Donna

Tears slide down Donna's face. She shakes her head, chiding herself it had been far too many years to still break down every year on this day. She pats the mule's neck before she climbs off and buries her face in his neck. She wonders what Gail would look like, what she'd think of Donna raising mules. Donna still daydreams about how things would have been so different if Gail hadn't died. Donna has always thought she was so tough, so strong, but she knows she'll never get over losing Gail. Donna has fought cancer, pretty much alone. She knows if Gail were still around she wouldn't have had to go through it alone. Some of the old gang from high school would probably have at least acted like they'd help. Problem was that Donna spent most of her time in Oklahoma, far away from California. Far away from too many memories.

Donna leads the mule back to the barn where his buddy, the molly mule nickers at him. Her thin arms lift the saddle and she carries it against a now nearly flat chest. She still grinned every time she got to carry something up close, the big chest gone, now. She wanted to have them cut down for decades, her shoulders and neck ached ever since they started getting so big in junior high school. Only good thing about cancer, she thinks. She got that one wish. She scratches the mule along his neck and messes with his ears. That was one thing she always does. She won't tolerate a mule who won't let you mess with the big ol' ears she loves. She stares at the long face and laughs out loud. "Folk say owners look like their pets. Guess that's true, now." Gail's granddaddy, Poppy, had always loved mules and she has learned why. Sometimes she got to go with Gail and her family over to Poppy's farm in Arkansas during summer vacations in Oklahoma and the girls got to mess with his big ol' mules. Besides, both her husbands had always said she was an ass. She grins at her own joke.

Donna notices the saggy skin hanging under her once muscular arms while she scoops grain into buckets. Granny bat-flaps, she had heard them called. She does miss being strong, misses being able to lift so much more, work so much more. She sinks onto a bale of hay and begins coughing while she watches the mules in their stalls. She tries to think of something besides Gail's death anniversary. Tries to think of something to be thankful for. The cowboy preacher where she attends church is always preaching on that, telling the congregation to remember everyone has blessings. She draws a circle in the hay dust with her small boot. *I know I should be thankful the cancer, the chemo, and the radiation has stopped my drinking.* She knows her excuses for drinking are the loss of Gail, the sexual abuse as a child, the loss of marriages, letting her children be raised by their daddy and a step-mama, just like her own mama did. That's all they are, excuses. There is a big difference between excuses and reasons. That was drilled into her as a kid. She came back, she saw her kids, not like her mama. Even when Donna was never without alcohol in her bloodstream she went to see them. She knows now the bottle didn't help her with any of life's troubles. Only she could help herself with that.

Donna feels the urge to cough rise again. She grimaces. She knows that the coughing is a sign of cancer. God, she hopes it hasn't come back. "Third time being the charm" rings in her head. She isn't gonna sweat the tests she's taken. If it is back, it is back, and it is meant to be.

PART SIX

The Reunion

Chapter Twenty-Three

Me

The pickup Buster and I are in climb down out of the foothills. We are using the old roads. We decided to fly for most of the trip, and rent a car for the last four hours of the trip. Midland is our closest airport and we decide to land in Reno rather than Sacramento. The rim country holds lots of memories for me. We had a forest permit and ran cattle near Mt. Lassen and the park when I was little. That was a headache due to the National Park status so Dad sold it, despite that country being some of the most beautiful country there ever was. It is still a pretty drive through the Sierras and past Lassen. The high county is verdant, snow still showing on the high peaks. We begin the rapid descent down from the 10,000 feet elevation. The highway winds its way down gradually from the fir and spruce trees to the ponderosa pine, then the foothill region. We pass the place where ranching neighbors gave me a baby shower, it burned down years ago. The big trees still stand around the blackened foundation. It was a bar, but also used for community gatherings.

Despite this being the land of so many creeks and rivers, and widespread valley irrigation, the country needs rain. The cheat grass is headed out early and the oaks and manzanita and digger pines are coated with a fine layer of dust. I see the river shimmering in the valley heat below when we round a curve. The orchards of pecans and walnuts are still growing along the river, and still look like a welcome oasis of green and cool, though alfalfa no longer grows under them. The old family dairy on the hill across the river is gone. Someone with money has built a big home to look down at the river and fields below.

We drive through the valley, through irrigated pieces of small acreages and through the subdivisions that have been laid and hatched in the middle of the pastures. Wagon wheels and white painted or split rail fences decorate most of the little places. When I was talking to Peggy a couple of weeks ago, she said it was the one town where everybody wanted to be a cowboy, and all the folks who moved there thought living there would make them cowboys. I now see what she meant. I see signs proclaiming so and so's ranch, and the place looks to be not even five acres. Wow. Things do change.

We pass the old paper mill and incinerator, long shut down. It was where so much of the population worked when I was a kid, and those men made a decent living for their families, despite being called "mill honkies". The kids attending valley schools always had to run inside when the stench was released like a cloud from the mill. Up ahead lies a shopping center/strip mall, and I was told there are now two stoplights in town. Wow, we were all excited when a four-way stop was put in. Then later while we were in high school the McDonalds was built in the big town fifteen miles away. Chains stores and restaurants didn't happen in these small self-sufficient towns.

We approach the main drag, originally the main highway through the length of the state, before the freeway was built. The old buildings are still there, including the two competing frosties or drive-ins as we called them. They are empty, paint peeling with boarded up windows. I think that's probably merciful, because they don't have to see that those fresh-faced kids have become gray haired grandparents. Let the buildings at least keep those memories of thirty-five cent burgers and fifteen cent cokes on trays brought by carhops and placed on car windows that cranked down. I don't think I will ever forget when both places started serving fried bean burritos. Most of the kids had never had them, their folks fearing the "furrin" Mexican food like burritos and tacos. My family cooked and ate Mexican food all my life, real Mexican. The only thing I was ever warned about was making sure tortillas were heated before eating them. Dad and Granddad doubted the gals patting them out washed their hands very well.

The banner is across the old tree lined street leading up the hill, proclaiming the reunion of the "Aggies and Cowboys." The school looks pretty much the same, the big irrigation canal still flowing on one side under the bridge. I smile as I remember that was a freshman's biggest fear, being thrown into that canal. The second biggest fear was being put in the trash can. This school was replaced by a big mega school built out in the country ten years after we all graduated. It is no longer a case of being from another town to attend a school in town. The new school belonged to no single town like it once did, leaving the country kids excluded from cliques formed from first grade. Our old high school has become a junior high.

We park in the shade under an old sycamore tree. I remember the balls being thrown and how bad they hurt when you got hit. Nowadays, a kid would probably go to jail for throwing them. The parking lot brings back lots of old memories, everything from eating in friends' cars with the rain pouring down the windows, to stealing some poor unsuspecting guy's Hostess cupcakes or Twinkies from the lunch his mama packed him. Some of the kids using the noon hour for steaming up the windows and giving the real meaning to a nooner. Heck, many of the boys' pickups had racks holding guns in the back window and every self-respecting boy had a pocketknife in his jeans. I wonder at the changes that have happened. I feel old, from a time long gone.

I can remember when I finally got to drive to school. It was the last week of my sophomore year. I got to drive Dad's fancy two or three tone blue Dodge pickup. I was surprised when I finally got permission to drive to school that it wasn't my mothers' fancy Chrysler Brougham with the eight-track player. I hated having older, stricter folks. They were the definition of conservative.

There is a fancy pickup with Oklahoma plates parked in the first row, and I bet Buster five bucks that it is Donna's. Buster and I get out and head toward the old ag buildings where banners saying *Welcome Back, Old Aggies* are hung. The big indentation is still there in the asphalt in front of the steps. It would always hold rain water that you had to jump over. These classrooms are a fair distance from the rest of the school, mobile additions placed far enough away for the shops and green houses to have plenty of space. More memories rush over me, memories of northern California torrential rain washing very black mascara and eye liner down my face while wallaby suede shoes got so wet the glue washed away leaving the soles flopping before we could get here to the agriculture buildings. The greenhouse is a reminder of how I learned to love growing things. We grew bedding plants, houseplants and vegetable starts we sold at the local grocery stores. I will never forget the couple of would-be hippy kids who grew pot plants among the flowers. I think they made more money than we did, at least until the teacher noticed the plants. The things you remember. I grin and shake my head.

I open the door and we step in. I stop and glance around quickly at the people before signing the book. There are some folks who look vaguely familiar. I sign my name and feel Buster nudge me. I hear a squeal and see a round-faced woman coming toward me hollering "Ginny! my God, it is Ginny!" Buster rolls his eyes, he didn't want to come and he didn't want me to go alone. He doesn't believe me when I say there are no old heart throbs waiting. He moved up here after I graduated and knows nothing about this old school and my classmates.

I realize the woman loudly screeching my name is Suzy, the eyes are still crinkled at the corners. Lord, she is so round. I cannot help but think of the old teapot poem and how she is really perfect for it now. I see the huge diamonds in her ears and catch a glimpse of more diamonds flashing on her wrists and chubby fingers as she throws her arms around me. I see Peggy look up, smile and head my way and realize Suzy's commotion has stopped all the conversations. Someone else yells "It is some of the smart ones, the ones who left California!" Weak laughter sounds from around the room. Wow.

Peggy steps out of the group and comes toward me, her arms in front of her ready for a hug. The long braid is still over her shoulder, just a different color. The silver strands make a pretty contrast to her dark eyes. I realize the old man beside her is Jim. He looks awful, gray-faced and thin. I hadn't heard he was ill, and I hope I cover the shock I feel at his appearance. I've always had a problem with my face showing what I'm thinking.

We move to a corner of the room and study each other's faces, searching for a remnant of the fresh teenagers we once were. I see the vestiges of eyes that once twinkled under heavy lids, surrounded by squint lines. I see perfect white dentures where teeth were once chew-stained, chipped, or maybe crooked. Slim waistlines are pretty much gone, though few of us are very heavy. There was far too much honesty in those bygone days, it would be labeled bullying now, I suppose. Getting fat was a fear every girl faced, right next to a giant pimple. The boys loved to tell us when we gained a single pound. It seems our bodies have become broader and shorter. I just hope our minds have widened with those shoulders and hips.

A tall, silver haired man slowly approaches our group and bows slightly before us. He reaches out to shake hands, give hugs he would never even have considered giving when we were students.

"Welcome back. This is the best group of students I ever had."

Someone giggles and says, "I think we were the last, too!" while another asks how sad is that we were his best class. We all know we were also one of the last classes he taught, but also some of the best achievers. Even back then rules had begun to change to make teaching harder. His strict methods would no longer be tolerated. And we were the last class to bring so many trophies home due to that stern manner of teaching that we feared and respected. You either played by the rules and did your best, or you weren't part of the team. Simple. There were no ribbons for just competing.

I see the trophy case on the far wall and think of how those trophies wouldn't be there without him. He taught us so much. Later I realized he was teaching us what our parents tried to teach us. Words from someone besides a parent are like a revelation. As if it was the first time we ever heard them. I wait for a chance to speak to him alone, to tell him how much good he put in my life, how he is one of those teachers who did make a difference. He taught me to push myself, taught me that I had real value. Something that didn't happen at my home.

I see some of the yay-whos have worn their FFA jackets. Some of the men are wearing old silver or nickel trophy buckles, and some of those buckles are halfway covered by bellies hanging over them. Many of the buckles are from the 1970s, the last time they rode.

A thin woman who looks like she stepped out of a magazine makes her way towards us. A trim man wearing a very nice quality hat is behind her, and she is holding his hand behind her back. I realize with a start it is Lori. The description of well-preserved comes to mind as she comes closer. She doesn't look like she did in high school, but she is sure trying to look younger. Her eyes are wrong, and her smile seems like her lips are swelled. The old description of bee-stung lips comes to mind. I see it is Tommy is who is being led behind her. His silver hair and starched clothing look classy, and he has aged well. Distinguished, I guess would be the right word.

Peggy smiles and says she's glad they could make it. Her smile is almost tender. I am puzzled. I heard they built a really nice place just a few miles away, why wouldn't they be able to make it? Why on earth would Peggy be soft toward Lori? Something is going on. Lori's smile she returns seems to tremble slightly. Wow.

Donna arrives, thinner than ever. I think she has new dentures and they aren't fitting right. Maybe it is just that she has no cheeks. Her face is far too thin, especially after being the rosy apple cheeked girl she was. We all try to not stare at each other and make small talk. When we're done with the meaningless chit chat Donna steps forward into the circle we've formed.

"Let's all go to the bar. You know, for old times' sake. If someone no longer drinks, we'll buy you a coke!"

Buster looks at me and I watch the others. Not a bad idea. And I am thinking some alcohol might loosen up some tongues so I can figure out what is going on with Lori and Peggy. Yeah, it is bugging me. I feel an electric current running through the group. It feels like a wet knee below cutoff jeans hitting an electric fence.

"We need to hang out a bit more, thank the folks who put all this together first," I say. I know what it is to be the one doing all the work for a party and be left feeling unappreciated and with the mess to clean up. I've learned some finesse and finally how to conduct myself. I don't want these local folks to think we hold ourselves above them.

After another half hour of greeting folks, thanking folks, and general mingling, we promise to see everyone the next day at the picnic at the river.

We escape to the parking lot and I hear Donna giggling like the teenager she was. She slaps me on the back and giggles again. Geez, like we just bs-ed our way out of class or something forty years ago. Guess some things really don't ever change. I grin, and feel my heart lift. Memories are good things. Sometimes.

The old sign is still on the front of the Old West styled building set back from the main drag, but a bit out of town. It had to be close to the auction yard, after all. Cattle deals and contracts often require alcohol to be completed. The parking lot still doesn't have much for lights in the back. I watch for beer bottles and chew cans, and I am surprised there aren't any. I hope we can still use the back door, that is if we can find it.

Geez, it is as if there's no lights at all.

A car pulls in and their headlights light up the back of the wooden board and bat building. Dang, I am still not seeing the door. I hear a chuckle and someone holler, "Are you all lost?" I recognize Tommy's voice and we stop. I hope it is him and not someone else. He comes up with Lori holding his arm, his phone lighting the way. She sure hangs onto him, I note.

"The old door got moved quite a while ago, when they took out the old poker room. Follow me, chillen'," Tommy says as he lights up the door.

We enter and the smell of whiskey and beer is almost overpowering. There's no smoke hanging heavy and thick like there used to be, and I wonder if that used to hide the booze smell. We find a table in the corner and grab the next table and its chairs to drag over to make a bigger table. I sink into one of the chairs and look around. There are young men in what we called "walking shorts" shooting pool. They have on sandals and scroungy t-shirts. Buster notices and grimaces. They sure wouldn't have been allowed in here or even wanted to be here when we were young. The fireplace is gone now. I can remember when it was often sprinkled with broken glass. Dusty wagon wheel replica chandeliers still provide the poor lighting. The same decades old Gorman prints are now yellowed but remain on the walls. Above the bar I see cowboy hats hung on pegs and what looks like plaques below each hat.

"What's everyone want to drink? I'll get this round," Buster says as he stands.

"I'll help you, I don't think that lil gal is gonna come over here." I jump up in a hurry. Buster is probably capable of carrying a tray without sneaking a drink, but I volunteer. I am also curious about the hats and want to see what the display is. I am not going to worry about him and drinking tonight. I am not his mother, and am so tired of the whole drinking game.

I look for an open space at the old scarred bar to squeeze between the stools to get where I can finally read the wooden signs under the hats. My heart sinks. They are the hats of folks we knew, some were big business folks, others were ranch or rodeo hands. All of them are gone now, but they have been given a place to hang their hats, forever. The hat of a one-time boyfriend in grade school. He was a Portuguese kid who married a woman with a passel of kids when he finally got his life together. He was pushing bulls down an alley when one of the bulls kicked the gate he was closing behind them. The blow stopped his heart, a twenty-six-year-old heart full of promise and love for kids he considered his own. The Grizzly hat of a ranch kid killed on his way to a dance out in the country. Big oak trees stop vehicles regardless of make, model or speed. The biggest businessman in town has his beautiful hat there with all the rest. It was custom made and far superior to the others. You can see that from here. His nephew's, Joey, battered, sweat-stained one hangs a couple rows over. Joey lost his battle with booze and cocaine and the country lost a damn good cowboy. There are a couple hats belonging to women. Rosie's is there, she was married to a much older man and made her living being a ditch rider, one of the last to actually ride a horse along the ditches. Her rawhide work and braiding helped put groceries on their battered table. It is a somber reminder of what this town once was and the folks who made it that way.

The drinks are sweating in front of us making small pools on the old tables, despite the coasters the barmaid finally brought over. Tommy clears his throat after looking around slowly. "Hasn't changed much, has it? Except maybe the clientele. We don't come in much anymore. Sure not what it used to be, and the cops hang around waiting for you to leave so they can pull you over. The county is pretty hungry and those kinda tickets sure help pad the coffers."

"Nothing is like it was. That's life," Donna says as she swirls her tumbler of cranberry juice and vodka. I wonder about the drink, Donna was supposed to have quit drinking a while ago. "I shoulda ordered what I usually drink. Guess I thought I was back in the old days, ordering fancy colored, sweet drinks. What the H? Don't know what I was thinking. Anyway, I saw you looking at the hats, Ginny. Only new thing here, besides the dumbass kids who come in here. Gail's hat should be up there. I told them so last time I came back. The dumb little girl asked me who she was. Said she'd never heard of her." Donna swallowed another mouthful and grimaced. I could feel her anger that the little gal didn't know who Gail was. I do have a hard time picturing one of Gail's colored hats up there next to the gray and black hats.

We are all quiet. I finally say we all know who Gail is, that's what matters. Donna stares at me and slowly nods. "Yeah, we sure as hell do." I offer to get Donna something else to drink and she nods and pushes the drink away and asks for a coke.

Peggy asks how things are going for Buster and me. We talk about kids, grandkids, cows and my nursery business. How we like where we live. Anything to get

Donna off the subject of Gail.

I am tired of talking about Buster and me. I change the subject. "Hey, Peg, you've earned quite a name for yourself with your art. I am so proud of you! See you are in all the big magazines, traveling to shows. How cool is that!" I smile at her across the table.

"Kinda surprising, if you ask the big-wigs from LA, Frisco and New York. They can't believe anyone from a small town, especially this little cow town, is capable of creating anything. Jim is doing well, too. Some of his clients are big money folks, and he is finally getting the recognition he deserves. It has been really hard on him to leave everything to his supervisor and foreman since he got sick. I think we've all done good." She smiles at each of us.

Tommy raises his glass and says, "To us! I don't think I need say anything more!"

We all clink our glasses and sip our drinks. I will wait to find out about Jim. I silently note that Lori is still holding Tommy's hand under the table. Her shoulders are tilted toward him are as if she is seeking protection, like he will cover her back. They've been together a long time, and appear to lack the confidence most long-time couples share. Something is definitely going on. I am not about to bring Bobby up. That's all I can think of that would maybe cause what I am seeing.

"So, how is life treating you, Suz?" Buster asks. He used to see Suzy at a lot of the rodeos further down the state when he was still riding. Suzy brightens when the spotlight lands on her, like she always has. Another thing that hasn't changed.

"I am doing good. Way better than what I ever thought I would be." She lifts the glass of Shirley Temple with the maraschino cherry and smiles. "I don't think anyone but an addict knows how hard it is to quit. I used it all, drugs and alcohol. I have a great therapist that costs me a fortune and a sponsor who keeps me lined out. I am grateful for that. My problems caused lots of folks so much pain, and cost me lots of relationships. Speaking of, I need to tell everyone of you all here at this table I am genuinely sorry for anything I ever did to hurt you due to those addictions." Suzy smiles and adds, "Except those things I did just because I am a butthead! You just have to live with those things!" We all laugh, breaking the tension that is strung like invisible wire around the table.

Tommy nods. "We are all proud of you and happy for you, Suz. I don't see a single damn angel sitting here. You can correct me if I am wrong. I don't know a person who hasn't had or has, a demon they've gone the rounds with. You beat that demon, girl!"

Suzy smiles a soft smile. "You all are good friends. I am finally getting back to where I am rebuilding relationships with my family. I can't ever take the past away. I can show them I am a new person and those old things won't happen anymore. Having money to help them out doesn't hurt a thing, either! Bad part is I sure eat good now, and my therapists says I am probably replacing my previous addictions with food. At least I ain't hurting anyone but me with eating."

I look at Tommy and measure my words. "So, I hear you and Lori are doing very well. Built a beautiful little ranch on the old place out of town." I nod at Lori, hoping they will talk about themselves. I was polite and called it a ranch, it is likely more of a horse property, I don't think Tommy's family ever had enough land to run cows.

Tommy turns to Lori and smiles. "Yep, we beat all the bets on staying married. Heck, I bet some of you all lost money on that! I remember, you could bet six days, six weeks, or six months on how long we'd stay together. We sure proved them wrong."

Peggy nods and smiles, and I see a flicker of something I can't read quickly cross Jim's face before he looks down. "No one said staying married was easy. I guess we are like you, too dang stubborn to give up and let those folks be right," Peggy laughs. Jim wiggles uncomfortably. Now, I know something is really up, with all of them, I think.

I look at the two couples across the big table and silently wonder what it is they are hiding. I spent far too many years with a husband who lived his life trying to hide things from me. One thing I've learned to do is read people like a book.

I notice Donna is quiet, with a faraway look in her eyes. I hope she isn't back to thinking about Gail. "Hey, Donna, you haven't said what you are up to, now. I saw some pictures, looks like you're still riding some. What are you doing with the mules?"

Donna looks at me and smiles. "Found out mules and I have a lot in common, Ginny. We're both stubborn as hell, built different from the sleeker, fancier models, but seem to have little mental retention. Oh, here's another thing. My last husband claimed that both mules and I have enough patience to wait all day for a chance to kick the hell out of you."

Donna lets the grin slowly fade away and continues. "In answer to your question, I see the kids when I come back, they don't come see me. You know, the karma thing we learned about way back when. Well, it has come around. Guess I am reaping what I sowed, as our folks would say."

The river seems a mile wide and appears as placid and peaceful as a river can with the same majestic oaks I grew up with lining its banks. The deadly undertows that have claimed so many lives over the years remain hidden. I remember watching the river at flood stage so often as a kid as we waited to cross it, seeing homes float down it along with giant trees. The old rickety bridges have all been replaced, bridges that would groan and sway when I got to ride in the cattle trucks loaded with calves for the sale yard. I know of several people who decided jumping into that river off the old bridges was a lot easier than shooting yourself. I hope folks have learned there's help out there now, counseling and stuff that wasn't around when we were kids. I break free from the hypnotic lure of the flowing water and look around. We have arrived early to the park, and see buildings have been added, along with additional acreage. Buster taps my shoulder and says we probably need to go over to a large gazebo type building we can see across the way. He allows me to get lost in memories, bringing me back when he figures I've seen and felt enough.

We head across the mowed grass full of clover and other pasture grasses. Kentucky blue grass lawns never last long here, the pasture grasses crowd them out. I shake my head at the oleander. There are cattle just across the fence. I remember when the freeways were planted with the deadly shrub and my daddy and granddaddy having a fit. Mama was never allowed to have one oleander in any of the places we lived. She loved her flowers, probably one of the few things I inherited from her. That and bony shins. The shins really sucked when I ran barrels, or when I do anything where a leg is exposed to injury.

I think we see Tommy unloading stuff from a shiny pickup. Buster is likely right. It would make sense to have some kind of cover for the picnic. As we get closer I see some of the folks from the reunion meeting. I really didn't want to come, and we foolishly promised we would after too many drinks the night before. Maybe that's why the cattle market usually stayed good here, it was too easy to agree to things in that bar.

Suzy is directing a van backing up to the pavilion, and I smell barbecue. I remember something from last night about her paying for a place to come cater the meat for the picnic. Buster and I stopped at the old grocery store and were happy to find they still sold cold fried chicken and had several kinds of tater salad. They also had packages of sliced tomatoes. The checker at the store even found a box to put our stuff in. We never go anywhere without contributing.

Turns out the caterer is someone we went to school with, a kid I don't remember too much. When I am in line getting my plate loaded, I mention the brisket smells good. He winks at me and tells me it is his daddy and granddaddy's adaption of California meets Texas barbecue. He uses a mixture of oak and mesquite. He is furnishing the pinto beans and coleslaw, too. Everything else is brought by the attendees. There's platters of watermelon and cantaloupe, and bowls of home-grown vegetables included in the huge line of food, everything from vegan dishes to nanner pudding, the real kind with calf slobbers on top. He wants to know how we like living where we do, he wants out of

California. He shakes his head as he tells us it sure ain't like it used to be. I ponder at how many folks say they want to leave California and wonder if they ever really will.

Buster and I find a table and are quickly joined by most of the old gang. I watch Suzy gnaw a drumstick down to the bone and then eat the cartilage caps off the end. She's found the chicken we have brought. I have to hide a giggle. She pays for the whole barbeque and goes after cold store-fried chicken. Someone asks Suzy if she is hungry, or if she's just polishing the bone. I remember when everyone ate chicken like that, it wasn't like it is nowadays where people take a bite or two and get another piece. Suzy mentions that the brisket is good and she thinks she saw a buttermilk pie, or that it might possibly be a chess pie. Peggy's daughter has joined us and asks what those are. I grin, it is common to see both kinds of pie at covered dish suppers where we live. I tell her to try them and I will send her the recipes if she likes them. My eyes fall on the watermelon. I can still hear the scolding when I was little and the dire warnings about spitting every single seed out. I was watched like a hawk to make sure I didn't swallow a single seed. I found out later that my granddaddy's aunt died at age three from choking to death on a watermelon seed. Amazing what family information you can stumble on nowadays. Some of these old stories explain why some old traditions were formed. I contemplate what the generation we raised is ignorant of, of how much doesn't get passed on.

"Robin, do you ever go to Texas or Oklahoma to compete? I know you have to have family back there?" I ask Peggy's daughter.

"Yes, I do. I haven't contacted any of them. Grandma Sandy was afraid they'd want to come out here to see Daddy. That isn't a problem any more with Pop gone. I may just do that."

I nod, and hold my peace. "Well, if you were to go to someone's house there, you'd probably get one of those pies. They're still an old-time favorite where we live.

Peggy looks up and smiles. "I need the recipe, Ginny. My daddy used to mention having them as a child." I nod and smile. Yeah, Peg would be one to honor the traditions, all right.

Some of our group moves to the benches by the river. While we eat, we make a plan that we'll gradually sneak away to get some privacy. I have to chuckle when Donna announces the plan. I wonder if the rest of the class thinks we are stuck up. Some of the kids believed that way back then. I don't think we were, we were highly competitive and set high standards we all adhered to. Today, we just want to catch up with the few folks we've kept in touch with over the years, though it was often off and on with a lot of years between.

Peggy has brought Jim and their plates to sit by us on the bench. Peggy is watching the river and comments how much the river is like life. Always flowing, deceptively peaceful with hidden dangers lurking. Flooding and raging and losing its way sometimes. That the key is to try and watch for when it runs amuck, and to not get sucked under that calm surface if you aren't careful.

I clear my throat and turn toward her. When did she get so philosophical? I change the subject a bit. "What's the deal with Lori, and with Tommy, I guess?"

Peggy looks at me and then looks way. "I don't know that I should talk out of school. I realize you all haven't been around, either, so you don't know."

I wait for her to look back at me. I see things in her profile I hadn't noticed before, or maybe she has let her guard down. The lines around her eyes are fine, as are the ones around her mouth. I get a feeling of hidden pain I hadn't sensed earlier. She has learned to wear a public face, I realize. Always smiling, always correct for the occasion. I will have to talk to her later. I am not really nosy, I am concerned.

"Let's go for a walk," she says. I watch her gracefully rise from her seat and I follow suite. We turn onto a patch that follows the river. We watch the river in silence as we walk a few minutes before she begins to speak.

"I think it would be better to talk to Lori, maybe even Tommy about their life, or I guess I should say problems or issues. You moved away and the last few years you were here you didn't exactly hang around. I know you were busy and had your own issues at that time. Lots of things happened after you left, some good, some not so good."

I remember noticing some things earlier, Jimmy's expression and his quick effort to hide it. I decide I will give Peggy a bit of a push, see if she will open up after I open up a bit myself. I nod and look at my old friend. "Yeah. Lots of stuff happens, it is life. Sure not what we dreamed of back when we were those invincible kids. Sometimes I look back and have to laugh how damn naive we were, so full of ourselves. At other times, how insecure we were. Afraid to try those wings we were granted. And then I think of Gail. And how it is so wrong of us to waste a damn minute, how she never had a chance to do anything. Folks say life is not fair. Well, I think most of the young folks nowadays don't have a clue just how unfair it is." I shake my head, and feel the tears that have formed.

Peggy stops and turns towards me. She grabs my shoulder and simply nods as she stares into my eyes. I know the wound is open and oozing. "Ginny. Nobody blames you for anything, not Donna, no one. We were damn stupid kids. We will never know why things happen. Please don't tell me you let a childish argument haunt you after forty years."

I shake my head, and deny that it does. It is only a half lie. It only bothers me when her name comes up. I can push it down, pretty far down, ninety percent of the time. Being back here has opened old wounds. I want to change the subject, even if it is to another tough subject. I have no idea why I begin telling her this. "There's things that happened other places, too. I will try to make a long, painful story short. Buster and I were one week from being divorced, had gone through all the court dates. Hell, I even have my maiden name back. I couldn't take the drinking. It was so out of hand. He'd lie about it. Hide beer everywhere; drive when he was drunk, all kinds of stupid crap. He'd sneak off to the bars, lie about that, too. Then, he graduated to messing around with women in the bar. His drinking almost cost us everything. The man I worshiped as a hero grew into an awful facade, my kids' daddy was a cheating lying ass."

Peggy stares at me and I feel the tears start rolling. "Oh, girl! I am so damn sorry. You never told any of us, never said a word. Just had to go on being tough ol' Ginny, no matter what. You were always that way, kept problems buried and never let anyone know. Damn, you can't keep doing that. Stress will kill you. They know that now."

"Yeah, I know firsthand about stress. Doctors said that's what caused my cancer. And probably caused the

TIAs I've had, in addition to hereditary genes."

"TIAs, cancer? What the hell? I hope you have some really good friends back there to rely on since you sure didn't give any of us the chance to be there for you." Peggy stares at her friend, torn between hurt and anger. "And you're still with the SOB? That's not the Ginny I knew!"

I wait a couple of minutes before I reply, trying to find the words to make the confession I really hadn't meant to share somehow make sense. "I was reminded by an old neighbor lady that when you tell folks just how awful the person you are married to makes you appear like a fool for staying married to them. It also makes it a lot harder if there's any chance of reconciliation, how do you take that bad of a person back? Then, there was also the kids to consider. Their father was just another big, overgrown kid, and unfortunately he is still their father."

Peggy stares at me. "So, you had no one to lean on, no place to go, back there? Why the hell didn't you come back here? You know you could have come to me." She sighs and shakes her head. "I am gonna go out on a limb and assume Buster got his crap together? That you somehow learned to live with his infidelities, his lack of responsibility and your kids were able to forgive him, as well? I mean you are their mother, and that is their mother's, and their lives the man messed around with."

I see hate beginning to burn in my friend's eyes. "Whoa, Peg. Things are better, much better. He got on the wagon, cleaned his act up. I stayed for the kids. I know you're never supposed to stay for your kids, and you have to look at how we were raised. Divorces only happened to the honky-tonking folks, and a whole bunch of them never bothered to divorce, they just carried on relationships in front of the entire bar crowd and half the town."

I don't tell her I am beginning to see the drag marks from the wagon Buster has been on for over fifteen years. He has an occasional glass of wine in social settings, but I know Buster better than he knows himself.

Lori and Tommy have invited us all to come to dinner while Buster and I are still here. Buster thinks it is so they can show off their place. We're the only ones who haven't seen it. The insecurities he will always have come up every once in a while. I don't comment, just tell him I want to see everyone while I can. Peggy says Lori loves to entertain now and has parties a few times a year, and they are often catered.

I wonder if I have anything to wear if this is a fancy shindig. I didn't pack clothes for anything formal. I ask Peggy about it and she says we will be fine. It will most likely be on the patio. We turn through the fancy gates leading up the tree-lined lane. The rolling hills are green from the irrigation system Tommy put in, and a few longhorn cows are enjoying the shade under the big spreading oaks. The house appears, set on a small rise. The old orchard sets to the side, slightly below the house while the barn and corral are on the other side. The builder did a good job. It fits into the surroundings, with the stone pillars on the wide front porch echoing the stone corral fences and the stonework on the barn Tommy's granddaddy built. It is a place I could easily see in the Texas Hill County and parts of Oklahoma, as well. We pull into a place under a tree and Tommy comes out to meet us. "You all come on. We're so happy you came!" Tommy leads us onto the porch and stops and turns. "I can't tell you all how much it meant to be able to get this place. Granddaddy bought it a very long time ago. He worked so hard to be able to get a place after coming out here. I know he'd be so proud to have family on it again. That was what he missed so much, the family he left behind." Tommy points at the pasture below. "I was even able to get all the land under irrigation, instead of just the creek side. We saved the old orchard he planted, and even found rock to use on the house to match the old corrals, though of course he didn't build those. You know that dates back to the poor ol' Chinese."

We admire the view and see the pride Tommy has in the place. He always took everything seriously, accepted responsibility full on, though he could sure party with the rest of us. He was a good friend, so many of my friends were boys back then. I learned early that females were often like cats, rubbing up and all friendly one minute and then bite and claw the crap out of you the next minute.

We enter through big double doors into the cool flag-stoned foyer. I can hear voices and some laughter towards the back of the house. He leads us through a living area where rich leather furniture rests on spotted cowhides strewn about, all facing toward a huge rock fireplace and mantle. Western art in heavy frames hang on golden oak paneled walls. Green plants complete the entire luxurious, yet cozy setting. I ask if any of the work is Peggy's, and he leads us over to a large painting of a cowboy pushing some pairs over a hill. Lupine and California poppies are mixed among the grass and the hill is dotted with oak trees. The frame alone is beautiful, layers of gilded oak and stamped leather. I see Peggy's signature in the corner of the painting. I am glad they're taking advantage of her talent and can afford to support her work. I am just so proud of her.

The view from the patio is gorgeous. Custom made fire-pits sit near each end of the long patio, set into the flagstone. Tables are set with a burlap-look cloth and western dishes. The cocktail and wine glasses are engraved with Tommy and Lori's brand. Fresh, country-styled flowers in white enameled pitchers are on each table. I see Lori is visiting with Peggy while they sip cocktails. Peggy smiles and Lori stands and comes to greet us. She gives me a big hug, and then grabs both my hands. "Sugar, I am so happy you came! Let me show you around." She guides me back through the engraved and square paned doors, and then she begins the tour of the house. The kitchen is a chef's dream. Every convenience and appliance was thought of and included in the design. The stainless steel is softened with old oak timbers and Talavera tile mixed with more of the flagstone. By the time we reach the master suite, my math of figuring the value of the house is nearing seven figures. Lori shows me the huge baths and dressing rooms adjoining the sweeping master bedroom. Lori tells me Tommy had the bedroom furniture specially made using some of the pecan trees from the old orchard. On a bureau, I see a photo of a young woman that looks familiar. I stop and stare at it, trying to place her.

"You don't know her." Lori says with a sigh. "I know you were thinking you should place her. That's our daughter." I feel my eyes widen in wonder and realize my mouth has fallen open, as well. I look at her in confusion. The girl is too old for me not to have known about, I can see that in the photo. My eyes travel back to the photo and I notice the photo next to it for the first time. It is of the same woman, with a small girl and a smaller boy sitting on her lap. Lori crosses her arms, and points at a chair, gesturing for me to sit down. "You probably need to sit to hear all this. Well, you remember when I said I was going to my aunt's when we were just out of school? I didn't go my aunt's, I went to a home for unwed mothers and stayed there 'til I gave birth. Yes, I was pregnant. My folks were mortified that I was pregnant. I wasn't ready for a baby. Hell, I couldn't take care of myself, you know that. One day I got a call from a young woman saying she was my daughter. I never dreamed the child would find me. I didn't even see the baby after I gave birth, had no idea if it was a boy or girl. The folks at the home insisted it was better for me to not hold the child, to not know if it was a boy or girl. I was assured the child was going to a home where the parents were wealthy and educated, and she'd be extremely well cared for.

"Of course, Tommy never knew about the baby, and I didn't know if it was his or that dumb ass from out of town I had seen a few times, I am ashamed to say. I really doubted it was Tommy's, we'd only been together that way once, and both of us knew it was a huge mistake. Tommy kept wanting to have a family. I couldn't bring myself to try to have a child when I had given one away. I had horrible guilt issues, I felt like having another child was placing no value on the child I already given birth to, -like children are this disposable thing. The doctors also told me after I had her that I'd probably not be able to have another. It was a very rough delivery. Tommy couldn't understand why I would avoid the conversation. I always had a thousand reasons to not have kids.

"When I arranged to meet her, there was no doubt who her daddy was, or that she was mine." Lori's voice wavers, but she continues. "I will never forget that moment, she smiled just like Tommy. And she is so much like my Granny! Good God, there was no denying she was our child." Lori wipes away a tear that has fallen.

Lori drew a big deep breath and went on. "Things ended up in a big, awful mess. Tommy saw from the credit card bill that I had lied about where I was going when I went to meet her. I had to spend the night, so I rented a room. Then he found out I wasn't where I said I'd be. I had made up a big story about where I was going since I had no idea if the whole thing was a scam to blackmail me or what. He accused me of cheating. Of course, I wasn't acting normal, either, so it isn't real surprising he'd think that. When I told him everything, he was shocked, to say the least. He was also angry as hell and hurt. He'd done everything he could for me, built this place, attended to every need or want he figured I'd ever had or have. He slowly forgave me, and is beginning to trust me a little again.

"Our daughter, I should say her name, Wynonna, is slowly learning about us, trying to figure things out. Her parents, the ones that raised her, had a hard time when Tommy and I became part of her life so she's learning how to have two sets of very different parents; and for her children, our grandchildren, to have so many grandparents. Our daughter is a single mother, and the father of the boy isn't in the picture at all. I am not sure the child's father knows he exists. Wynonna was with the girl's father for a while. I sometimes wonder if our daughter doesn't resent me for not doing what she did, raising a child on her own. She doesn't really understand those were different times. We were raised in a different world. No way would my parents have supported or helped me raise a bastard child. You can't forget that Tommy and I also are distant cousins, adding to the whole mess. They'd have died of embarrassment first, before owning up I had an illegitimate child from a distant cousin! Mama spent her life trying to erase that whole Okie stigma away, it likely would have killed her."

We hear Peggy calling for us and I try to digest all that's happened. We were pretty typical teenagers, I guess. I can see Lori has paid dearly for her indiscretions. I think we've all grown up and learned to be better people. At least I hope that. We meet Peggy near the living room, and I mention how beautiful her painting is. Lori smiles and says she's going on ahead to her guests on the patio, leaving Peggy and I studying the painting.

I am still reeling from the revelation Lori just

shared with me, and try to think of something to say to Peggy. "Friend, I have to tell you how awed I am by you and your work. You were able to make a fairy tale life out of a Cinderella stepmother story, except she wasn't your stepmother. I'm sorry for being so honest, yet that's one thing life has taught me. Honesty and reality are the best. I don't mean to disrespect your mama, I'm sure she thought she was doing what she figured was best for you. Who knows, maybe Sandy drove you to perfection," I add, trying to soften my harsh opinion and words. I don't think I will ever learn finesse.

"No, Ginny, you are being honest. And correct. I allowed way too much, had things happen that never should have because she had instilled in me I wasn't worth much. My life hasn't been a fairy tale, either. The only part that fits a fairy tale is the nasty ol' stepmother, my real mother in my case. Let's sit down for a minute here, where it is quiet. We haven't had much time together, alone time, at least."

I settle down into one of the buttery leather chairs and Peggy selects a seat next to me. "I didn't mean you had everything easy, I shouldn't have said anything at all. That's me, talking when I don't know what I am talking about. I'm sorry, Peg."

"You can't know everything, you escaped this small town, and all the drama. And the friends we share didn't tell you, I see. Like you, infidelity became an issue for me, too. It about broke my heart, especially when you find out it is someone who's supposed to be your new best friend messing around with your husband. I was foolish and had to go see for myself. That probably came from my mom's philosophy that I should hurt myself. Yes, I've been in therapy and that's what I've been told, that she wanted me to hurt myself as much as she hurt me. And his affair just supported my mother's belief that I was a loser, that I couldn't even keep a man."

"Oh, Peggy. That's bull, you know that. You weren't the one failing, it was him."

"I am only telling you because you weren't here. If you had been, Jim would probably be dead," she laughed.

She knows I am not tolerant, especially when I was younger. Like last year younger. No, really, I have learned quite a bit of patience. Probably not enough, though.

Peggy continues. "The worst part was my mother pretty much telling me I wasn't attractive enough to hold a man to begin with. So, according to her I needed to stop the foolish painting and focus on my husband. You know, like the 1950s. Have a drink ready for him when he gets home, never let him see me without makeup or God forbid, in dirty clothes I worked in. If I had worked harder in bed he wouldn't have strayed," she said.

I feel more disgust than ever for Sandy, but keep my mouth shut. Damn that woman. Peggy studies me for a minute before going on. "Jim had realized his affair with the gal I thought was a good friend did nothing but use the both of us. She was looking for a Sugar Daddy to deliver her out of the life she had. It ended abruptly when he realized what folks were saying about her and his foolishness was true. She used me to get to him. Jim never could stand a user.

"Jim came over to surprise me and ask if I'd take him back and it just happened my mother was there. Jim came up on the porch and heard her telling me everything I just told you, about me being a piss-poor wife. When he heard her, he threw the door open and told her to get the hell out of his house, no one talked about his wife that way. You should've seen my mother's face." Peggy giggles.

Donna is standing and staring out at the horses grazing below when Peg and I return to the patio. I go stand beside her. I can feel her solitude, her feeling all alone though she is in the midst of her oldest friends. "Pretty view, isn't it, Donna?" I ask. Donna mumbles something and turns to me, a smile now on her face.

The smile doesn't show in her eyes.

"Mind if we walk down to the creek, Tommy?" I ask over my shoulder as I give Donna a slight shove in that direction.

"Sure, you all watch out for snakes. I've killed a couple lately. If you see that ol' Longhorn bull, he's fine. Don't worry about him. He loves to lay down there in the shade. He's more liable to get up to beg for cake than anything."

I gently lay my arm across Donna's thin shoulders and say something about going to see if there are fish or salamanders. We make our way down to the creek, watching ahead in the grass for any kind of movement. I have my good boots on, and Donna has on low-topped shoes. I finally break the silence.

"What's up? Something goin' on you want to share?" I wait, giving her plenty of time to gather her thoughts.

She looks around and sighs. "You know all that partying we did as kids? And you know full well I extended that lifestyle decades after that. Like Suzy, just not so much with the drugs. I guess crap does eventually come around. Now the docs say the drinking, partying, not getting enough sleep, all of it increases your chance of cancer. They figured out the smoking does years ago. No one ever mentioned the rest of it. The good part of getting breast cancer is that I finally got to have those back breaking jugs cut off. Most folks know about the bad parts, they've had someone they knew fighting cancer, or they've fought it themselves. I view it as actually have a benefit."

I stare at the pasture around us and swallow hard. "Donna, I know we're supposed to listen to the damn professionals about health and medicine. Problem is that they change everything every couple of years. From what we should eat, to how much water we should drink, to how much exercise we need. We don't know what to believe, whether to get a flu shot, or whether kids should even get vaccinations. Well, I will tell you this. A bunch of these young folks haven't seen their childhood friends get TB from the family milk cow, or had family crippled from polio. Or had family diagnosed with bad hearts from childhood incidents of rheumatic fever and other stuff.

"I think a person is gonna get what a person is gonna get, I don't think there's always a cause. You probably are thinking I am a dumb ass since I haven't had to fight cancer like you have. I did have a little bout with the big C, I was lucky, they got it all. I've watched too many friends and family with it. And you're right when you say fight. You either fight it with all you have or you just give up and let it win. Sometimes it wins, anyway."

Donna nods. "Being back here with you once again after so many, many years is really something. It makes my heart fill up, both with good memories and the sad ones. We left here, and I think we're better for it. Lots of our old buddies said they'd leave, couldn't wait to get out of here. They ended up staying. Look at so many of 'em, just plain sorry folks. Let's go back and visit, we're probably being rude."

I know Donna isn't going to tell me what's going on right now. She has managed to skirt the entire issue. I try to push back the worry, and hope I see her again before we head back home.

Suzy is one of a couple of the group not drinking, but is the person who someone observing the group would peg as being three sheets to the wind. She is still the loud, pushy, gal she always was. Her tummy shakes with laughter and her eyes are crinkled into her face. She swats at Tommy. The only difference is that would have been a punch when we were kids. I hear laughter about Suzy getting on a horse. I start to grab a beer and change my mind. I grab a bottle of water instead and sidle up to hear what's so funny.

Suzy leans back to look at me and Tommy reaches over and tugs her hair. She rolls her eyes and swats him again. "Ginny, they're making fun of me because I am too dang fat to even get on a horse! Can you believe this horse crap?" She giggles at her pun. "I did try to get on one a few months ago to try it out for one of the kids, my niece. Geez, I can't even get this ol' leg that high to get into the stirrup. Imagine that. All Around Cowgirl, Hollywood stunt girl can't haul her big fanny up into the saddle anymore. Maybe they should write that in our reunion book.

"I am really glad you and Buster, and Donna came

home. I am serious. I sure miss you guys. I am glad you didn't see the really bad things that happened, too. It was pretty ugly for a while, a long while, really. I am sure someone has shared most of it with you. I am here to say I did hit the bottom of that barrel and every stave in it on the way down. Then I hit so hard I knocked the bottom out of it. I am damned lucky to be here. It is funny how that stuff you were taught as kids comes back when you really need it. I am so thankful my grandparents made me go to church whenever we weren't on the road, and made me learn all those Bible verses. That faith gets me through. It gives me hope. I remember thinking they were such hicks. I thank God every day for them, and for giving me something to lean on. I would never have made it through without that ol' time faith.

"Drugs made me into someone I didn't even know, and someone I didn't want to know. I can blame lots of things, and some people, for pushing me into where I felt like I had to have them. Truth is, there is no excuse. It was up to me. And I just flat out was not strong enough to resist the temptation. Then I got to the point I wanted to keep in that land of make believe, and never leave it. I had it made, that's the saddest part. I was contracted all over for my new act and I was getting a good foothold in Hollywood doing stunts and doubling for some of the actresses. I knew I was losing my kids and my parents respect, to say nothing of everybody else. It got where I lost all my contracts and Hollywood stopped calling. When I figured there was no sense in going on I tried to OD on purpose. I'd already ODed a few times, so it wasn't that big a deal. Then I did it on purpose and left a note.

When I woke up in the hospital to those pain-filled faces around me, I knew I had to do something. I had a hard time believing they still loved me. That was incredible to me. I didn't feel worthy of their love. I was reminded more importantly that God still loved me.

"So, now my only addictions seem to be for food and spending money. I can't make up for the things I did to my kids. We are slowly rebuilding a relationship. I am now financially able to help some folks. I am giving back after all the years of taking. Hell, I even did good things for my folks before they passed away. I realized they just really wanted the best for me, they didn't know things did not have to be that hard. The way our folks were raised and what they went through made them what they were. Those were different times."

I look around at the group and think back to how long I've known these people. The ties are deep, and strong. Our folks knew each other before we were born. Some of them made the long, painful trip to California together. Others met when they ended up in the little town so similar to where they grew up, recognizing voices and expressions, manners from where they came from. Some of our parents did better than others, the connection kept them together, even if they hadn't spoken in years. Let one of the folks labeled as an Okie die, let one of them or their family members get hurt and watch the old customs come out. Quietly visiting and writing checks to those who needed it. Covered dishes and desserts came out by the droves. Women sat with women, in hospitals, at funeral parlors, and at homes. Men showed up to do chores. I wonder how much of that still happens here. I am glad I live where those things are still practiced.

I look over at Buster and he gives me a slight nod. I slowly stand and smile. "Much as I hate it, we need to call it a night. Lori and Tommy, I can't thank you enough for such a lovely evening, for getting us all together. Buster and I need to start our trip back home to the ranch tomorrow."

Tommy stands. "Nope, you just sit down. The night is young even if we ain't anymore! We don't do this very damn often. Please stay. Lord knows when we will see you again, when we will all be together again." I look over at Buster and he reluctantly nods.

There is a feeling of relaxation that seems to slide over everyone. Like a deep, silent sigh. Glasses are refilled and legs stretch. I see Donna staring off and go stand beside her. I slide a chair next to her, and sit down.

"Hey, lady. I hope you are realizing you're with some of the best people in the world here. Folks who love you and always will."

She turns to look at me and I see the sheen of tears in her eyes when she replies. "It doesn't matter where we live. Remember, I don't live here, either. That doesn't matter. It's where we came from that matters. We're the last of our kind. At least we were smart enough to go when the getting was good!"

I laugh and give her a squeeze. She shudders and sobs rack her thin frame. I wrap both arms around her, holding her. Lori and Peggy have quietly arrived to gather round us, they silently left the table where Suzy is regaling the guys with stories. After a few minutes of just holding her tight I ask Donna what the matter is, warning her not to try to test an old BSer. "Not much, except the damn cancer is back. Third time is a charm, ain't it?" I am silent not wanting to say the wrong thing. Dear God. Donna is all alone. I swallow the choking feeling in my throat.

"Do the kids know?" I ask.

"Nope and they don't need to know. They don't really care, and I sure as hell ain't staying here. I've got my place back in Oklahoma, even have a few kin folks around. I've been through this before." I place one finger under Donna's chin and gently turn her face toward me. "You aren't going through this alone, again. You'd never have gone through it by yourself if we'd known. You can come stay with us, bring your mules and dogs, whatever. Or, I will come and stay at your place. You're not doing this alone. I damn well mean it."

Peggy clears her throat before she joins in. "No, ma'am, you are not. I can take care of you, too. You might want to consider getting treatment and doctors here. Jim's doing better and I have made the decision that Mom needs to go to an assisted living place to be happy. She sure as hell ain't happy with me. And I doubt if she'll ever be happy, truthfully. Surprise, surprise. So, anyway, I sure would like you to come stay with us. They've got a lot better doctors here, now, too,"

Suzy reaches for her coke and glances over. She knows something is going on. She comes over to join us. Peggy gently reaches down and strokes Donna's hair. "Honey, we are all here for you. You do need to know that." Lori and I exchange looks over Donna's head. Both of us have tears ready to fall.

Suzy is looking at each of us and finally asks what the Sam Hill is going on. I quietly tell her that Donna's cancer has returned. Suzy manages to squeeze next to Donna. "Well, I was needing a vacation. Guess I will be coming out your way, probably have to stay for quite a while. Maybe forever." Suzy winks at me. Donna tries to laugh through her tears and ends up snorting. We all join in laughing, hugging each other through our tears.

"Your choice lady, where you will be. We will be there, no matter where it is." Peggy swipes at Donna playfully.

I get up to find another glass of wine. My heart is

so full it aches.

I wonder about Suzy's offer to go back to Oklahoma, if that won't be an issue with her fairly new husband. She and Donna are discussing Donna's mules and horses, and Suzy says maybe she'll even try and get horseback again. Peggy starts talking about new cancer treatments. I slide up and quietly ask Suzy about being gone from home so far away and so long. I am sure all of us are silently thinking Donna's treatments will likely entail several rounds of chemo and radiation in addition to surgery. I remind her I can sure go to Donna's or take Donna home with us and get her animals to take to our place. Suzy looks up and meets my eyes. "It won't be any trouble. I didn't want to rain on everyone's parade this weekend, but dumbass had me served with divorce papers, his cute little secretary hand delivered them to me at the house. So, it will be good to get away, and I really do need to look up some of my folk's kin while I am back there. That will give us both something to do, besides watching me try to get back in shape!

"And, I am gonna tell you all something, I am tired of California, and what it has become. These last few days have shown me how much we've changed, become California-ized. Being around Donna and you brought back memories, and hearing you all talk about being back there just clinched my decision. I feel like I am fixing to go home. There. Hear that? I've only been around you all a couple of days and I am saying 'fixing' and 'you all'. I think my grandparents would be proud, even if my folks wouldn't be."

I am silent, wondering if these two OCD people will find strength in each other. Donna must have read my mind. She shakes her head at me and says "We will be okay, we will watch out for each other and be there for each other. It will give me a chance to help Suzy, too."

I figure they won't be that far from me. I will drive a few hours to check on them when I need a break. I need to get Peggy to come out, and Lori, too. I decide I need to hold a reunion, back in Texas. Donna and Suzy can have one after that in Oklahoma. They all need to come out, their husbands, children, grandchildren. They need to see where their families came from, and have someone ask them who their people are. They need to understand where the Okie's daughters came from, and why some of them have returned.

CPSIA information can be obtained
at www.ICGtesting.com
Printed in the USA
FSHW021859060721
82847FS

9 781633 635210